ASHLEY JOHNSON

Sister Assassins: Sinister Seduction

Forged in Fire

First published by Forever Seven Press 2025

Copyright © 2025 by Ashley Johnson

All rights reserved. No part of this publication may be reproduced, stored or transmitted in any form or by any means, electronic, mechanical, photocopying, recording, scanning, or otherwise without written permission from the publisher. It is illegal to copy this book, post it to a website, or distribute it by any other means without permission.

This novel is entirely a work of fiction. The names, characters and incidents portrayed in it are the work of the author's imagination. Any resemblance to actual persons, living or dead, events or localities is entirely coincidental.

Ashley Johnson asserts the moral right to be identified as the author of this work.

Designations used by companies to distinguish their products are often claimed as trademarks. All brand names and product names used in this book and on its cover are trade names, service marks, trademarks and registered trademarks of their respective owners. The publishers and the book are not associated with any product or vendor mentioned in this book. None of the companies referenced within the book have endorsed the book.

This story contains mature themes including graphic violence, sexual content, manipulation, murder, and psychological instability. Reader discretion is strongly advised.

First edition

ISBN: 979-8-9856989-8-5

Editing by Shelley Lopez
Cover art by Megan Katsanevakis

This book was professionally typeset on Reedsy.
Find out more at reedsy.com

Contents

Tempting Desires	Isabella	1
Blindsided	Isabella	5
Detective Ryde Me	Eli	13
The Itch	Isabella	20
The one he's hunting| Isabella	25
No Mistakes, No Patterns	Eli	30
The Cracks Form	Isabella	37
Dinner and Delicious Deception	Eli	42
Office Hours	Isabella	51
Unreachable	Isabella	58
Crimson Ready	Isabella	63
Something About Alexis	Isabella	66
Red Smear	Isabella	71
Suspect	Eli	75
Ghosts	Isabella	80
You Ruin Me |Isabella	83
Whispers In The Dark	Isabella	88
Loose Threads	Eli	93
Tangled Patterns	Eli	98
Fractures |Isabella	103
Blurred Lines	Eli	108
Soft and Sharp	Eli	113
Kiss me, Kill me	Isabella	118
The Way I Burn	Isabella	123

Bruises Don't Lie | Isabella	131
The Tell | Eli	139
Sloppy Seconds | Isabella	146
Too Quiet | Eli	152
Between The Line and The Lie | Eli	159
Everything Is Quiet Expect The Cracks | Isabella	164
Saved or Signed Death Warrant | Isabella	168
The Thin Blue Line | Eli	174
Motive, Means, and Morris | Isabella	179
The Tipping Point | Alexis	183
Like Nothing Ever Happened | Isabella	187
Like Freedom | Isabella	192
Still Bleeding | Isabella	196
The Ones Who Walk Away | Eli	201
Epilogue | Isabella	206
Note to My Readers	208
Note from the author	209

Tempting Desires | Isabella

The bell rang, signaling the end of another exhausting day at Jefferson High School. I sighed with relief, grateful for the respite from the chaos of my classroom. I loved my job, but the days took their toll.

Leaving the familiar halls behind, I slipped out of the school, eager to shake off the weight of responsibility for a few hours. My footsteps echoed on the pavement as I made my way to my car. I knew exactly where I needed to go.

The bar's entrance greeted me with the familiar aroma of stale beer and the distant murmur of conversation. I slid onto a stool at the counter and ordered a glass of red wine, hoping it would loosen my tense muscles.

My smooth, deep brown skin akin to sun-kissed bronze glowed. My ebony curls, cascaded down my shoulders in untamed waves—much like my wild spirit.

Dressed in a form-fitting black dress that hugged my curves, I exuded strength and confidence. The sleeveless design revealed toned arms, a testament to my dedication to my hours at the gym.

As I sipped my wine, my eyes roamed the room, scanning the different faces. Some bore the weariness of long days, while others reveled in the escape of camaraderie. In the corner, a live band played a soulful melody, adding to the bar's magnetic allure.

Then, I saw him.

Tall, dark, and exuding confidence that was almost tangible. His eyes, deep and enigmatic, were intriguing. His rugged charm and mischievous smirk sent a thrill through my veins.

I smelled the arrogance from across the room.

That's when I knew. He would be my prize tonight. I swung my legs to the side, crossing them slowly, deliberately. I didn't look at him, but I could feel his gaze burning.

Within seconds, someone leaned in beside me.

"Is this seat taken?"

"By you," I said smoothly, holding out my hand. "I'm Bell."

He took my hand, brushing his lips across my knuckles. "Michael."

"You seem lost, sweetheart," he murmured, his hand sliding onto my leg.

Rage flared hot in my veins. I took a slow sip of my wine, forcing the fire inside me to cool.

"Lost?" I echoed, tilting my head. "Oh no, I know exactly where I am. I'm just enjoying the view."

His smirk widened. "I'm flattered. The view is pretty great, isn't it?"

I swallowed a scoff. "I was talking about the bar." I gestured toward the liquor display, feigning indifference as I took another sip.

He chuckled. "Touché. So, what brings you here tonight?"

I leaned in slightly, suppressing the urge to snap his fingers for touching me without permission.

"Well, I heard there was a charming man at the bar who thinks he's king of the world. I just had to see for myself."

"King of the world? Nah," he corrected, his smirk deepening. "More like the emperor."

That made me laugh. At least he was showing me the real him right away.

"Emperor? That's quite the upgrade. What's your empire?"

He raised a brow. "Oh, I'm an expert in…everything."

I rolled my eyes. "Everything? Wow, you must be quite the Renaissance man."

"Well, I do have my talents," he replied, lowering his voice.

I matched his tone, barely a whisper. "Talents, you say? Do enlighten me."

He grazed his fingers further up my thigh, leaning in closer. "I could tell you, but then I'd have to show you."

I turned fully toward him, forcing his hand to drop from my leg. Thank God.

"Well, I suppose I'll have to stick around and see if that's true."

His grin was all challenge. "Please, be my guest."

The conversation played like a well-rehearsed dance, each word laced with innuendo and unspoken desire. The more we talked, the more I despised him. He thought he was a prize to be won, that he could take whatever he wanted.

Well, welcome to Bell.

He took my hand and led me to the dance floor, moving in sync with the pulse of the music. The rhythm wrapped around us.

In the heat of the moment, I felt alive. Almost forgot my task. Almost.

The song ended. We left the bar, hands intertwined, seeking a more intimate escape.

Outside, he moved toward the parking lot, but I had other

plans.

"This way," I purred, smirking as I tugged him toward the alley beside the bar.

He slammed me against the brick wall and crushed his mouth against mine. Heat pooled low in my stomach at the aggression. I lifted my right leg, wrapping it around his waist. His hands found my throat and pressed, sending a thrill through me.

My nails dug into his sides, clawing at his skin. The hunger inside me twisted and coiled, eager for the moment I craved.

He bit my neck. I heard the telltale sound of a zipper. He adjusted his stance, his pants slipping lower.

I smiled wide. There's my cue.

My hand slid between us, slipping into my bra where my precious key lay hidden. The one that was hollow with the concealed blade inside.

With practiced precision, I pierced his jugular.

The gasp. The frantic grasp at his throat. The wobbling step backward, his unfastened pants hanging off his hips.

I adjusted my dress as he crumpled to the ground.

I turned and walked away from the alley, confident that he would draw his last breath before I hit the street.

The thrill coursed through me, saturating every nerve.

Yes. It would be a good week.

Blindsided | Isabella

I woke up on Saturday morning feeling good—real good. A deep, satisfying calm settled over me, and the lingering sweetness of my latest indulgence coated my tongue like honey. I grinned, stretching lazily, basking in the afterglow of my personal high.

Then, a sharp crack stung my lips.

Damn.

I swung a hand to my mouth, wincing at the dryness. Throwing back the covers, I scoured the room for my slippers. One was kicked under the bed, the other in the middle of the floor. Slipping them on, I padded to the bathroom, my reflection in the mirror confirming the culprit—lips as dry as the Sahara.

"Alexa, what time is it?" I called out, rubbing in a layer of lip balm.

"The time is 11:16 a.m.," the AI responded.

Shit.

I was meeting Alexis at 12:30 for brunch, which meant I had exactly 40 minutes to get my ass in gear.

Standing before my full-length mirror, I selected a breezy royal blue sundress, pairing it with a wide-brimmed hat and nude beige sandals that crisscrossed up my ankles. As I misted my curls with water, shaping them to perfection, my phone buzzed with a Face Time call.

"Hey girl," I answered, holding the phone up.

"You still at home? Girl, why ain't you on your way?" Alexis' exaggerated exasperation made me chuckle.

"I am literally walking out the door right now," I said, snatching my keys and slipping on my sunglasses. "See?" I interrupted her before she could drag me further. "Leaving now. I'll see you soon, love you." I hung up with a series of kissing noises before heading out.

I pulled up to Brunchin' and spotted Alexis' car, parking beside her. Sliding my sunglasses off as I entered, I met the host's gaze.

Tall, broad-shouldered, and filling out that polo shirt in a way that did dangerous things to my thoughts. His golden eyes locked onto mine, and for a split second, that familiar itch sparked in my veins—a slow, smoldering burn.

"Hello, ma'am. How many?" he asked, voice smooth, polite.

Hmm. Polite, young, and well-mannered. The itch fizzled out. Not for me.

"I should have a friend already here," I said, rising on my tiptoes to scan the room before spotting Alexis.

"Ah, there she is," I pointed.

He smiled, stepping aside. "Go right ahead."

I sauntered over to Alexis, raising a brow at the nearly finished mimosa in front of her.

"So, you started drinking without me?"

"Bitch, you're late, and I couldn't wait," she grinned, pushing a fresh mimosa toward me.

I glanced at my watch. "It's 12:40. You act like I had you sitting here for an hour."

Taking a sip, I recognized the splash of mango juice—my regular.

"How have you been, though?" I asked, picking up the menu. "Last time we spoke, your man was trippin'. What happened with him?"

Alexis sucked her teeth, rolling her eyes. "Absolutely nothing. But I've moved on already. I met a guy named Jabari Ryder."

I raised a brow. "Okay, girl. Wasted no time, huh?"

The waitress arrived, taking our orders.

Alexis shifted in her seat, biting her lip before rushing out, "And I might have invited him and his brother Eli to brunch today because you need a man too."

I stilled. "Alexis," I chastised. "You did what?"

"Bell, listen, just hear me out," she pleaded, hands flailing. "Jabari asked me to brunch, but I told him no because I already had plans with you. He offered to come later for drinks instead, so we'd have our time first. Sweet, right?"

I narrowed my eyes. "And then?"

"And then," she continued, stuffing a bite of food into her mouth before mumbling, "he said he'd bring his brother because you ain't no third wheel, and you need a man. It's been ages, Bell."

Alexis peeked at me.

Lord knows I didn't have time or space for a man. But what's done was done.

"You've already invited them. You act like I can say no now."

Her grin widened. "Girl, his name is Eli Ryder, and he is FINE." She snatched her phone, scrolling excitedly. "I made

Jabari send me a picture."

Before I could react, a deep baritone voice interrupted. "Ladies."

Alexis and I turned in unison. A dangerously sexy man stood before us.

"Jabari," Alexis beamed as he leaned down to kiss her cheek. He turned to me. "Bell, I assume? This is my brother, Eli."

Good. God.

When Eli stepped aside, the air seemed to shift.

His presence commanded the room, quiet strength radiating from every inch of his towering frame. His dark, smooth skin glowed under the soft lighting, warmth emanating from him like a slow-burning fire.

His deep-set, polished onyx eyes took me in, scanning every inch. When he spoke, his voice was rich, velvety, with just the right amount of gravel to make my stomach clench.

"Hello, Alexis. Bell," he greeted, extending a large, well-sculpted hand.

I reached for it, my fingers brushing his, and instantly scanned my body for the itch.

Please, no.

I just got relief. I shouldn't feel it. Not now.

"Yes," I replied, forcing a smile. "I'm Bell."

His strong, chiseled features, broad nose, and well-maintained beard only added to his allure. His thick curls framed his face naturally.

He was confident. Commanding.

A man who knew his worth without needing to prove it.

He wore a crisp white button-down, rolled sleeves revealing muscular forearms, fitted dark jeans, and suede desert boots.

"Please, sit," I offered. I glanced at Alexis, raising a brow. She grinned and mouthed, "I told you."

It dawned on me then.

Our table for two had become a table for four.

"You get blindsided into this too?" Eli asked, his voice smooth as silk.

Damn.

* * *

Eli

This woman is gorgeous.

Her laughter is soft, melodic, wrapping around me like silk. When I ask if she was forced into this setup too, she giggles. "Is it that obvious?"

Something about her voice has me caught in its grip, smooth and rich, curling around me like warm smoke. I run a hand through my hair, feeling a strange pull I can't shake. What the hell?

I meet her dark, mesmerizing eyes. "I was racking my brain for a way to break the ice. Aren't these things always awkward?"

She leans forward, propping her elbow on the table, angling herself toward me. "Alexis didn't tell me we'd have company until she saw you guys walking in." She side-eyes her friend before rolling her eyes dramatically.

I chuckle. Damn, she's fine. The kind of fine that demands attention without trying. The kind of woman who knows she's stunning but doesn't rely on it to get her way. That kind of confidence is lethal.

"Well, Bell, tell me what you do?"

Her attention shifts back to me. "I'm a teacher," she says before holding up a hand like she's about to give a full disclaimer. "Yes, I know the educational system is a mess. Yes, I have a million ideas on how to fix it. No, I don't want to talk about it, and I take no responsibility for every crazy teacher you see on the internet."

I lean back, amused. "Damn, a whole dissertation, huh?"

She laughs, and I swear it's one of the best sounds I've heard in a while. "I can't tell you how many pointless conversations I get dragged into after someone finds out I'm a teacher." She pauses before flipping the question. "What about you? Anything as controversial as me?"

Her eyes lock onto mine, waiting.

Shit.

Her gaze narrows playfully. "Ahh, it has to be. You done got all quiet."

I exhale through my nose, smirking. "I'm a detective."

Her brows lift slightly. "Hold on now," she says, holding up a finger. "Not just some beat cop, right?"

I shake my head. "I've graduated from that."

I can practically see the wheels turning in her head. "What department? Narcotics?"

Something flickers in her eyes. There's history there. What is it? Law enforcement in general? Or detectives specifically?

"Homicide," I answer, studying her closely.

She notices my scrutiny and smirks. "Don't go detective-ing me. That's off-limits."

"Are you easy to read?" I challenge.

"When I want to be." Her voice dips lower as she leans in slightly. "You reading me now, Detective Ryder?"

The way she says my name sends a jolt through me, tightening my grip on my glass. This woman is dangerous. The way she moves, the way she speaks—she knows exactly what she's doing. It's calculated. But is it a game or just who she is?

I shift in my seat, clearing my throat. "What are some things you enjoy?"

She relaxes, a knowing smile playing at her lips.

Damn, those lips. Lush, plump, glistening with some two-toned gloss that has my full attention. I want to taste them, wondering how they'd feel against mine.

"I enjoy things like museums and plays," she says, tilting her head. "I'm big on musicals. Like, sing-every-word big. What about you?"

I shake my head. "I really don't do much outside of work." I pause, then add, "Maybe that isn't true. I just don't do anything consistently. I'm not big on going out. Today, Jabari and I were supposed to do one of his monthly 'brotherly bonding' events." I make air quotes, smirking. "He makes me go so we can 'stay connected.'"

Bell watches me closely. Her eyes flicker back and forth like she's debating something.

"What's on your mind?" I ask.

She narrows her gaze. "Are you detective-ing me again?"

I chuckle. "Of course not."

"So you don't watch TV? No musicals?" She changes the subject.

"You want to hear me sing?" I clear my throat, leaning in slightly. Her eyes gleam with amusement.

"How does a bastard," I start, smoothly delivering the first verse.

She bursts into laughter. "Hamilton doesn't count! You have to pick a song with actual singing in it. That was cheating."

I smirk. "A musical is a musical."

She scoffs. "Alexis!" She calls out, turning toward her friend. "If he says he can sing and then starts rapping Hamilton, does that count?"

"Hell naw," Alexis co-signs without missing a beat.

Bell turns back to me, triumphant.

I shake my head, grinning. "You said musicals, not singing in general."

"Hamilton has singing in it," she counters.

"Not from Lin-Manuel," I shoot back. "Now you can't tell me with a straight face that dude can sing."

She presses her lips together, struggling to hold back laughter. "He is very talented," she replies diplomatically.

"Oh no, that's not what I said." I chuckle.

Every time she smiles, the restaurant seems a little brighter.

The more we talk, the more I realize how easily I'm sinking into her energy. We're laughing, challenging each other, and it feels good. Time moves differently around her, and for the first time in a long while, I don't feel the weight of work pressing down on me. There's something about her, something magnetic.

And it's dangerous.

Brunch turns into an unforgettable encounter, and as we say our goodbyes, I know I'm in for some shit.

Because I don't want this to end. And that? That's a problem.

Detective Ryde Me | Eli

The stack of case files on my desk was already high enough to make me want to pour myself a drink, but when Captain Matthews sauntered in and tossed another thick folder on top, my patience wore thin.

"You've got another one," he announced in that dry, no-nonsense tone. "This one getting the best of you, huh?"

I leaned back in my chair, jaw tightening. "There's no connection, no ties, no similarities—except for the stab wound to the neck. Nothing is connecting these cases."

"We have a serial killer, Ryder," he said, like he was stating a fact, not an assumption.

I shook my head. "I don't think they're connected. I don't believe it's a serial killer."

He raised a brow. "Do you not believe it because you can't solve it?"

My eyes narrowed, but he just threw his hands up in mock surrender. "All I'm saying is, if we do have a serial killer, you need to find him, quick. These neck wound cases are piling up. You've got five on your desk right now."

"It's not a serial killer," I muttered. "You just have me working five cases simultaneously."

Matthews chuckled and shook his head, amusement gleaming in his eyes. "So it's me overworking you, huh? Yeah, okay."

He turned and walked away, leaving me to stare down at the fresh case file. Another body. Another stab wound. But something wasn't adding up. If it was a serial, there'd be a pattern. A calling card. A motive. But all I had were bodies with slit throats and no discernible connection.

"Ryder, get moving," Matthews barked from down the hall. "They're waiting on you to move the body!"

I sighed, dragging a hand down my face. "Buried the lead, huh?"

"You're a pro. Why do I have to tell you that?"

The scene outside the bar was chaotic. A small crowd had gathered, murmuring in hushed voices behind the yellow tape. An officer was locked in a heated conversation with a woman whose expression screamed frustration.

"When will I have my bar back? I'm losing money!" she hollered as I walked up.

"Ryder," a uniformed officer nodded, lifting the tape so I could duck under.

"What do we got?" I asked Sergeant Toligbly.

"Male, identified as Michael Hoover, age thirty, lives over in Bluegarby."

I raised a brow. "Bluegarby? What's he doing over here slumming?"

"Good question." Toligbly sighed. "Guy was stabbed right in the throat. Clean through the carotid artery."

I crouched next to the body, eyes narrowing. Hoover's pants were unzipped. A pool of blood had already started to congeal beneath him.

"His pants," I noted, shooting a glance at Toligbly.

He shrugged. "Hey, whatever people do in their spare time

is on them."

"Any cameras?" I asked, scanning the alley.

"Nope. And the owner up front is giving my guys hell."

I pushed to my feet and walked toward the entrance. Sure enough, the woman from earlier was still running her mouth.

"Ma'am," I said, approaching her with a forced calm. "I need to ask you a few questions."

She crossed her arms over her chest and cocked a hip. "What?"

"Who found the body?"

"I did," she snapped. "This is my place. Y'all shut it down. When will I be able to operate again?"

"We're working on that. Did you know the victim?"

She scoffed. "You think I know everyone who comes in here? I wasn't even working last night. My manager was."

I clenched my jaw. "Where is your manager?"

"Monica is home. I work the day shift."

"Do you have a number for Monica?"

"Of course I do. It's in the office, in the building you won't let me go into."

I sighed, motioning toward the entrance. "I'll escort you. Let's get that number."

Inside, she led me through the dimly lit bar to a small office in the back. She rummaged around a cluttered desk, but I wasn't paying attention. My wrist buzzed, and when I glanced down, my screen lit up with a picture of Bell—lace bra, panties, and a teasing smile.

My jaw clenched. My dick twitched against my zipper.

Goddamn.

"Like what you see, Daddy?" the owner's voice dragged me back to reality.

I snapped my gaze up. Her smirk was predatory, as she arched her back just enough to make a point.

Annoyed, I exhaled. "You got the number?"

Her expression soured. With a dramatic eye roll, she snatched a scrap of paper, crumpled it, and tossed it at me.

I caught it midair and gave her a tight-lipped smile. "Someone will be in touch."

As I walked out, her voice followed. "What about my bar?"

"Fuck your bar," I muttered, stepping back into the humid air.

The Medical Examiner's van had arrived. I crouched beside the body once again, scanning for anything that stood out.

"What can you tell me?" I asked the M.E.

"This guy was stabbed," he deadpanned.

I rolled my eyes. "Wait for the report like everyone else."

I lowered my voice. "Does this wound look similar to the others?"

The examiner arched a brow. "You think we got a serial?"

I rubbed my jaw. "Captain does."

"I'll call you later with a preliminary opinion."

Back at the station, Mary, our receptionist, gave me a knowing smile.

"Hey, Mary."

"You have a visitor," she said, nodding toward the waiting area.

I sighed, but when I turned, my breath caught.

Bell.

Sitting with her legs crossed, black heels laced up her calves, her skin glowing in a way that made my hands twitch. When she stood, the dress hugged her waist, accentuating every damn curve. Her lips were glossed, her eyes glinting.

I swallowed hard, clearing my throat.

"Mmm," I hummed, eyes trailing over her.

Her lips curled. "Do you have somewhere private we can talk?"

My pulse kicked up. I nodded, leading her toward the conference room, closing the door behind us.

"What do I owe this surprise?" I asked, curiosity lacing my tone.

She didn't answer. Instead, she stepped closer, grabbed my hand, and guided me toward the opposite side of the table. Without breaking eye contact, her fingers worked at my belt, my zipper sliding down with ease.

My brows shot up. "Bell, we can't do this here."

She smirked. "You sure?"

Hell.

I should've stopped her. I really should have. But the second she dropped to her knees, I knew—

I was absolutely fucked.

"Bell, really. We cannot do this here."

She swivels my chair so that she is hidden by the table from the door and grabs my dick. Squeezing it. she stroked my length.

I gasp as I watch her stick her tongue out and lick the pre cum off the head, still with her eyes locked on mine.

"Holy shit." My eyes close and she devours my dick down to the hilt in one slurp.

I grab a handful of thick curls and pull. Her head jerks back as she grins. "Still want me to stop?" she asks.

I respond by pushing her head down and listen to her gag as she takes me entirely in her mouth. She grabs my balls and squeezes as her teeth and tongue rake up and down.

I tense when I feel her index finger press past my ass.

"Whoa," I say.

She looks at me as she presses her finger in, while she squeezes and rolls my balls and then deep throats me at the same time.

"Holy shit," I gritted through my teeth.

My eyes roll back in my head and I lace both hands in her hair and grip tight.

"I'm coming, baby." I gasp as her head bobs up and down. I feel the finger going deeper in my ass as the tension in my body increases until my hand clenches her hair, my thighs tense, and my seed burst.

I grunt as my eyes bulge out of my head. She slurps up every drop and then wipes her face, smiling.

I damn near lose my mind when there's a knock at the door and I see the knob twisting.

Bell, who is already partially under the table, turns a little so the table conceals her entirely.

She planned for this, I think as I roll the chair closer to the table's edge, only thing visible is from the chest up.

"Hey man, your phone keeps ringing. What the hell you doing in here?" Jason asks. Spencer Jason and I work as partners on some cases. I would call him my friend. He's the only one I see outside of work.

"I just needed a moment. Here I come," I say, proud my voice came out leveled.

He sticks his head in further and looks around. With one eyebrow raised he asks, "In an empty room?"

"I said here I come, dude."

Jason narrowed his eyes and then shook his head before backing out of the room.

"Close the damn door," I bellowed after him.

I roll the chair back and Bell stands up, rubbing the front of her leg. I grab my drawers and jeans from around my ankles and pull them up, standing to finish the zipper and button.

"Will I see you later?" she asks.

I cup her chin, unable to resist.

"I don't know how late I be," I say. "How about this weekend?"

I see disappointment flash over her face but it's gone the next second. A smile slips in place. "Okay, I see you then. Call me with details. okay?" She leans in and kisses me, then turns and walks out.

I head to the bathroom and clean up. I pass Jason's desk, who sees Bell come out of the office, and then looks back at and smiles.

I wave my head at him in a shooing motion and turn the opposite direction for the bathroom.

The Itch | Isabella

My body is starting to itch.

Not the kind of itch that can be scratched, not the surface-level discomfort of a bug bite or an allergic reaction. No, this is deeper, coursing under my skin like an electric current, buzzing with the weight of need. A need that has been left unsatisfied for too long. It's been three weeks since my last one, and the withdrawal is clawing at me, sinking its teeth into my every thought.

Eli.

I hadn't planned for him, hadn't anticipated that a man like him could shake my equilibrium. But here he is, infecting my mind, disrupting my balance. He is an anchor. A detective. The worst possible attachment for someone like me.

I slam my palm against the steering wheel, a guttural growl escaping my throat. The car's dashboard clock flashes 3 p.m., glaring at me, taunting me with the reminder of how long I've resisted.

Enough.

I make my decision in an instant. I need to hunt. Now.

I exit the car, enter my home, and lock the door behind me. One final check—no phone, no watch. I can't afford distractions or breadcrumbs leading back to me. A blade in the shape of a key is nestled securely between my breasts, hidden in a sewn-in slot of my workout top. I grabbed my hoodie and hat and was out the door.

By the time I reach the park, my pulse is already racing—not from exertion, but anticipation. The familiar trails stretch ahead of me, their paths winding through dense trees, shadowed corners. I weave through them, the rhythm of my feet against the dirt mimicking the pulse of hunger inside me. The sun is beginning to set, but the heat still lingers, clinging to my skin like a second layer.

Five minutes of searching, I see him.

A lone runner, stretching on a bench. Perfect.

I jog past him, my smile flirtatious, my wave casual. Then I stop, panting as if exhausted, my hands resting on my knees as I bend forward, my form on full display.

I don't have to look to know he's watching.

When I glance back, his attention is locked on me, his own stretching forgotten. A slow smile spreads across my face.

Hooked.

The anticipation morphs into a delicious thrill as I continue deeper into the trails. I want to be secluded, hidden from prying eyes but still within reach. I know these paths well—I have hunted here before.

He follows, just as I knew he would.

"I haven't been up this way before," he comments as he approaches, his voice light. "Good trail."

I tilt my head, smiling. "What made you come this way today?"

He shrugs. "Pretty girl influenced me."

I take a step closer, lowering my voice. "You followed me

deep into the woods. I could be dangerous."

He laughs, but there's an edge of uncertainty. Not enough to turn him away, but enough to make him thrill at the possibility.

"We're far out here, huh? No one around to see," he muses.

We stop and lean against a thicket of trees. I let my fingers trail from his collarbone down to his chest, feeling the heat of his skin through his thin shirt. The air between us thickens, and for a moment, neither of us moves, neither of us breathes. My senses sharpen, the hunger peaking, wrapping around me like a vice.

His hands settle on my waist, pulling me flush against him. "You up for this? Out here?"

I cock my head to the side, pressing my hips forward just enough to let him feel me. His smirk grows, cocky, expectant. "I guess that's my answer," he mutters before his mouth crashes against mine.

I try—really try—to let myself get lost in it, to let the buildup consume me. But all I can think about is how this kiss isn't as good as Eli's. How his touch isn't as firm. How his scent doesn't make my head spin the same way.

Eli is ruining this for me.

Frustration simmers beneath my skin as I break the kiss, grabbing his hand and pulling him further down the secluded path and to anther hidden tree. I push down my shorts, presenting myself in a way that guarantees no refusal.

He fumbles with his shorts, his eagerness making him clumsy. He grips my hips and plunges in, grunting his satisfaction.

I try to focus. I try to feel.

But it's not enough.

The build-up, the sweet, slow climb to euphoria—it isn't there. His panting, the sloppy rhythm of his movements, does nothing for me.

I am losing my release, and that is unacceptable.

The moment he gasps, his pleasure spilling over, I step forward, pivoting before his mess can touch me. He grips himself, stroking out the last of his orgasm. His head tips back, his body loose.

I feel nothing.

And that, more than anything, makes my decision for me.

I step forward, my fingers curling around the key between my breasts. In one swift motion, I flip the blade open and plunge it into his throat.

The feeling is dull, empty. No satisfaction, no rush. Just irritation.

I don't bother watching him fall. Instead, I turn, breaking into a sprint, weaving through the trees until I merge with the more populated trails. No one pays me any attention. I blend in. I am just another runner, finishing her workout.

By the time I reach home, I am seething.

This was supposed to satisfy me. It was supposed to be my release, my euphoria. And yet, I feel nothing. Nothing but the intrusive thoughts of Eli.

I slam the door behind me, stripping off my clothes as I stalk toward the bathroom. The hot water runs, the scent of vanilla and coconut filling the air. I sink into the tub, my body aching in ways I can't place.

I need to figure this out. I need to fix this.

I either need to get rid of Eli, or I need to find a way to hunt with him in my life. Because I will not deny my nature.

My fingers trail absently along my collarbone as my mind drifts back, back to my first.

Connor.

He never should have died. It was an accident. A game taken too far.

But that accident had given me my first taste of true euphoria, and I have been chasing that high ever since.

Until today.

And that?

That is unacceptable.

I stare at my reflection in the bathwater, my fingers curling into fists. The hunger is still there, gnawing at me, whispering.

Eli is a problem.

And I don't leave problems unsolved.

The one he's hunting| Isabella

It's been a long day.
The kind of day that clings to your skin, weighing you down with every exhausting second. The kind of day where I wish I had just stayed in bed, called in sick, and let the world move on without me. But I didn't. Instead, I dragged myself, pushing forward even when every fiber of my being screamed for rest. The kids at school were especially relentless today, their energy grating against my last nerve like sandpaper on raw skin.

By the time I trudged out of the building, the weight of fatigue settled deep in my bones.

My phone dings from the bottom of my bag. I switch my work bag to my other arm, wedging my coffee cup between my side and my elbow as I dig around like a desperate scavenger. The phone stops ringing before I can reach it.

"Damn it." Whoever it was will have to wait.

"Hey Google, what are my notifications?" I ask as I settle into my car and hook up my Bluetooth.

"You have a missed call from Alexis."

Figures.

"Hey Google, call Alexis."

Her phone rings so long I think she might not answer, but

just before the last ring, she picks up.

"Bout' time you called me back," she snaps playfully.

I roll my eyes. "Girl, you called me literally five minutes ago. What's up, Queen?"

"Ohh," she sings, dragging out the word. "Queen, huh?"

"Yeah, Drama Queen," I retort.

She sucks her teeth. "I am not a drama queen! I could've been dying or something."

I snort. "Yeah, not a drama queen at all. What's up though?"

"What are you doing?" she asks.

"On my way home."

"Home?" she screeches. "Let's do happy hour or something."

I groan dramatically. "Alexis, I can't. I'm so worn out today. I need to go to sleep."

"Sleep?" she mimics. "Come on, Bella. It's Thursday, you know all the foooooinee men will be there."

"You go," I say, shaking my head. "And wait—what about Jabari?"

"What about him?" she asks.

"Aren't you seeing him?"

"Yeah," she admits, and I wait for her to continue. "Sooooo," I prod.

"I'm not only seeing him," she says breezily. "Come on, Bella. You know a bitch can't be tied down."

I roll my eyes. "Well, you have fun with all those foooooinee men. I am going home. I'm exhausted, girl."

She clicks her tongue. "What, you got Eli waiting for you?"

I smirk. "Do I sense jealousy?"

"Yes, I am jealous!" she squeals. "You are dismissing your best friend for some man."

"I didn't invite Eli over, girl. I literally just want to go home and soak."

By the time we hang up, I'm pulling into my driveway. Just as I shift into park, my car's Bluetooth blares a ringtone through the speakers.

Eli - Detective splashes across the screen.

I sigh before answering. "Hey, you."

"Whoa," he says, concern laced in his voice. "You sound exhausted. Long day?"

"Yes. I should've called in today. It started off bad. I just need to get some rest."

"Let me come up and take care of you," he says smoothly. "And you can't say no because I'm already here."

I jerk my head around, and sure enough, he's pulling into my driveway. "How did you know I'd be home?"

"I wasn't stalking your schedule or anything," he teases, then hangs up before I can respond.

I shake my head, stepping out of my car as he does the same.

The man looks damn good, and even in my exhaustion, I can't help but take a second to appreciate him. His dark jeans hug his frame just right, his button-up shirt slightly wrinkled from the drive.

I pop the trunk. "I just need to grab my stuff," I say as I reach for my bags. "I don't know how much fun I'll be. I'm really exhausted."

"You don't need to entertain me," he says, taking the bags from my hands before I can protest. "Let me take care of you."

He shuts the trunk and turns to me. "You don't need any of this stuff tonight. Unplug from work for just one evening."

I try to fight the grin that spreads across my face, but it's useless. I must look like a love struck fool because he chuckles, shaking his head. "Good. Let's go."

His hand finds the small of my back, guiding me inside.

Later that night, after a warm bath and a much-needed change into my softest pajamas, I make my way to the kitchen. The delicious aroma of something rich and savory fills the air. My stomach growls.

"Mmm, what is that?" I ask as I enter the kitchen.

Eli looks up from the stove, a smirk on his lips. "It's a surprise. Come and sit down."

As we eat, I notice the tension in his eyes.

"What's wrong?" I ask, setting down my fork.

"There's a killer out there," he admits, his voice rough. "A calculated one. No connections between the victims, no trace evidence. It's like they just…vanish into thin air after the kill."

I shift slightly in my seat. "No leads at all?"

He exhales sharply, running a hand over his face. "Nothing. It's like they know exactly how to avoid leaving anything behind. No fingerprints, no DNA, no security footage. Just bodies left behind like…offerings."

A chill runs down my spine. "That's terrifying."

His jaw tightens. "It's infuriating. The precision, the control—it's not random. This person is careful, meticulous. They don't just kill—they plan, they study."

I swallow. "Do you think they'll do it again?"

He nods. "Without a doubt."

I hesitate, my fingers tightening around my glass. "What kind of victims?"

"All men. Different walks of life, different backgrounds. No common threads except how they were killed. A single stab to the carotid artery. Quick. Clean."

I force myself to exhale. "You'll catch them, Eli."

His eyes darken, frustration flickering beneath the surface.

"I have to."

Silence settles between us. I lace my fingers through his, pressing my thumb over his knuckle.

For tonight, that's all he needs. And for tonight, I let myself pretend that I'm just Isabella, and not the one he's hunting.

No Mistakes, No Patterns | Eli

The station smelled like burnt coffee and desperation. I sat at my desk, staring at the board in front of me, red string crisscrossing between photographs, locations, and timestamps.

The killer was precise. Efficient. No struggle, no mess. Just a single stab to the carotid artery, a wound so clean it could have been surgical. Five men, different backgrounds, different lives, all dead in the exact same way. No connection, no motive, no damn fingerprints. It was like they had just stepped into the wrong moment at the wrong time.

I rubbed my temples, my fingers pressing against the ever-present headache that had been sitting behind my eyes for weeks.

"Ryder," my partner, Jason Spencer, called from his desk. "You've been staring at that board for hours. You expecting it to start talking back?"

I shot him a glare. "Funny."

He leaned back in his chair, crossing his arms. "Look, man. You're running in circles. This guy—whoever he is—isn't making mistakes. No patterns, no slip-ups. Either he's a ghost, or he know how we work."

"Yeah," I sighed. I was starting to think there was some type of inside knowledge. It has to be."

Jason stood and walked over, scanning the photos. "If there's no connection between the victims, maybe you're looking at this wrong. What if the connection isn't *who* they are, but *where* they were?"

I exhaled slowly and leaned forward, flipping through the files again.

"Michael Hoover, found in an alley behind Monroe's Bar. Christopher Day, jogging trail near Eastwood Park. Jaylen Rhodes, hotel parking lot. Jerome Vasquez, abandoned lot off Sixth. Anthony Wright, behind a strip club on West 14th."

I frowned. The locations didn't overlap in any obvious way, but Jason had a point. "Were these random dumps or was this guy just leaving bodies wherever."

Jason nodded. "Might be a comfort zone."

I grabbed a marker and circled the locations on the board. Five deaths. Five locations. All isolated enough that there wouldn't be immediate witnesses, but not so remote that it would look staged.

"What about timestamps?" Spencer asked. "Any commonality there?"

I started checking the reports. "Hoover was found around 2 a.m. Day, early morning, just before sunrise. Rhodes, late night, around eleven. Vasquez, early evening. Wright, just past midnight."

Jason whistled. "Killer's got no set time. Not a creature of habit."

"Or they're testing," I murmured, my mind clicking through possibilities. "Trying different time windows to see what works best. To see when they're least likely to be caught."

Jason crossed his arms. "That's someone who's learning, not

someone who's careless."

I nodded.

A knock at my desk pulled my attention. Captain Matthews stood there, arms crossed. "Ryder, Spencer. We got another one. Found twenty minutes ago. Same MO."

I felt my stomach tighten. "Location?"

"Riverside Park. Jogging trail."

My mind was already running scenarios. The killer had struck again, and that meant I was still two steps behind.

Jason and I grabbed our coats quickly. The ride over was tense, Jason tapping his fingers against the dashboard. "We're missing something," he muttered. "There's got to be a pattern."

I wasn't so sure anymore.

When we arrived, the scene was quiet, but the tension in the air was thick. The body was covered with a sheet, but the blood had already started to soak through. I crouched beside it as the forensics team worked, my eyes scanning everything.

Same wound. Same precision.

I stood, looking around. If the killer had left this body here. We were far enough off the more populated paths for privacy. No one would have wandered by here.

A shiver ran down my spine as my gut twisted. Somewhere in the shadows, I could feel it.

The next morning, I barely slept. I kept thinking about that body—how it was arranged..

By the time I got to the precinct, Spencer had already pulled surveillance footage from cameras near Riverside Park.

"I got something," he said the moment I walked in.

I took the tablet from his hands, pressing play on the footage. The timestamp read **2:15 p.m.** The camera caught movement— someone jogging past the camera, then a bicyclist, then a woman pushing a stroller. Nothing out of the ordinary. Nothing that screamed 'killer'.

Then there was a flash—a reflection off something metallic, maybe a watch, maybe a phone screen catching the sun. A split-second gleam, and then it was gone.

As if they knew the camera was there.

I rewound the footage, leaning in. "Damn it. Nothing conclusive. Just people living their lives."

Spencer sighed. "Yeah, but why?"

I stared at the screen, watching the figure continue down the jogging path, blending effortlessly into the late afternoon crowd. Then, just as they passed a lamppost, something changed—someone else, a man in a gray hoodie, hesitated, glanced over his shoulder, then picked up his pace. Not unusual, but something about the way he moved, like he was trying to act normal but failing, caught my attention. Something gnawed at me, something primal.

We ran the footage through enhancement software. The image sharpened, and this time, the man in the gray hoodie came into clearer focus. Late twenties, average height, wearing a ball cap under the hood. He wasn't running, but he wasn't strolling either. Something in his posture screamed tension, awareness.

Spencer squinted at the screen. "The thing is, I thought this dude looked kind of skinny. Look at the way he is built."

I leaned in. "So, what are you saying? You think this is a woman?" I asked in disbelief. "How do we even know this is the person we are looking for. How do we find this person?"

Spencer zoomed in again, this time on the ball cap barely visible under the hood. "Hold up, freeze that," he said. I did. The resolution was trash, the pixels muddy, but a shape emerged... a slanted white triangle. Or maybe a roof line. Hard to tell.

"Is that a logo?" I asked.

"Could be." Spencer leaned closer. "Looks like the kind Ridge & Co. prints on the uniforms for the buildings they manage."

My brows lifted. Ridge & Co. owned half the downtown apartment complexes. Cheap, aging units with the same faded geometric logo slapped on every cap, jacket, and maintenance vest.

"It's thin," Spencer admitted, "but maintenance crews jog all the time. Before or after shifts. And that building on Sycamore has a service entrance right behind the park."

It wasn't a smoking gun. Hell, it wasn't even a warm one. But if the person in the hoodie worked on one of those buildings, or lived in one, or even cut through the area regularly. It gave us a place to watch.

"Grab your coat," I said, pushing back from the desk. "We'll sit on Sycamore. If our ghost belongs to that building, they'll show eventually."

And that was how we ended up on a cramped downtown street an hour later, staring at a nondescript apartment complex and waiting for a gray hoodie to walk out its back door.

I glanced down at my phone as it buzzed in my lap. *Isabella*.

Isabella: *What are you doing, Detective?*

I smirked, thumb tapping back a reply.

Eli: *Sitting on my ass, watching for a guy who might be a waste of my damn time.*

Another buzz.

Isabella: *Sounds boring. Maybe I should help you unwind later?*

I exhaled, shifting slightly in my seat.

Eli: *Depends. How exactly would you help?*

A pause. Then a photo came through—a teasing glimpse of skin, just enough to send a jolt straight through my body.

Spencer side-eyed me. "You sexting in the middle of a stakeout?"

I locked the screen and cleared my throat. "None of your damn business."

Spencer snorted. "Jesus. Hope she's worth the hard-on while we're tracking a potential murderer."

I rolled my eyes. "Shut up and watch the door."

An hour passed. The city hummed around us, car horns, distant sirens, the occasional shouts from a nearby alley. Then, the door to the complex opened. A man in a gray hoodie stepped out, hands stuffed in his pockets.

Spencer straightened. "That's him."

"Look like a woman to you?" I asked. The build really didn't match, but that looked like the hoodie.

Kessler moved with purpose but didn't seem nervous. He didn't scan his surroundings or hesitate—just walked down the street like he had somewhere to be.

"Let's tail him," I said.

We followed from a distance. Kessler didn't seem to notice, didn't turn around once. He walked four blocks, then slipped into a coffee shop.

Jason frowned. "Guy's not acting like someone who knows we're on him."

I nodded, stepping out of the car. "Let's go say hello."

Inside, Kessler was ordering a black coffee, staring at the menu like he had all the time in the world. When he turned, his gaze landed on us.

His fingers clenched around his coffee cup. His jaw tightened. He hesitated for just a second too long before stepping toward the exit.

Spencer blocked his path. "Daniel Kessler?"

His eyes darted between us. "Who's asking?"

I pulled out my badge. "Detective Ryder. We've got a few questions for you."

Kessler licked his lips, nodding, but his body language screamed flight.

And I was ready for it.

The Cracks Form | Isabella

The gym was nearly empty; the echo of my punching bag thuds bouncing off the walls in a steady rhythm. My knuckles were raw beneath the wraps, sweat dripping from my forehead, jaw clenched. I needed the ache. The sting. I needed to remind myself I was still in control.

But control was slipping.

Eli had tangled himself into my mind. Into my skin. Every time he touched me, it carved a deeper mark into the part of me that used to be unreachable. And worse, he was getting closer. Close enough to ruin everything if I wasn't careful.

The blade nestled inside the fake lip key in my gym bag burned like a warning against my side. I stared at the bag, heart hammering. I hadn't used it in over a week. Unheard of.

Not since *him*.

I couldn't lose my edge. I had to prove I still owned this hunger. So tonight, I would feed. Cleanly. Efficiently. *Unemotionally.*

I slipped out the side door, hoodie up, body coiled like a spring. The streets were alive, music and chatter bleeding from the bars. It was Friday night. Neon lights flickered over passing cars; laughter spilled from a rooftop bar, and across the street. College kids stumbled out of a pizza place arguing over ranch versus blue cheese.

Perfect hunting ground.

It didn't take long. A finance bro type with whiskey breath and expensive cologne cornered me outside a club, mistaking my silence for coyness. He followed me to the alley. Predictable.

"You sure this is what you want, baby?" He asked, smug.

I smiled.

"Oh, definitely."

The blade slid out fast. But just as I moved to strike—

His phone rang. A loud, grating ringtone that shattered the moment.

"Shit, one sec."

He stepped back, fumbling with his phone.

"Yo, what up! Nah, just out here with this *bad* chick. Hold up—"

I vanished into the shadows before he turned around.

Heart racing. Jaw locked.

Sloppy.

That word echoed in my skull as I walked home, ignoring the buzz of the city around me. The flashing lights, the people, the noise—none of it could drown out the roaring inside me.

Back at my house, I paced like a caged animal. The itch was worse now. The failed kill, the unfinished high—it pulsed under my skin like fire ants.

I opened the fridge, staring but seeing nothing. Slammed it shut. Yanked open the freezer. Slammed that.

Shit

My mind wasn't focused; I was sloppy. Were there cameras? I don't know, I wasn't careful. Did anyone see us go into the alley? I don't know, I wasn't looking. I know better.

The house was silent except for the hum of the air conditioning, and yet it felt like the walls were pressing in. I sat on the couch, curling my knees to my chest. I felt the key pressing against my breast. The cool of the metal reminded me of how close I came to an absolute disaster. My breathing came in short bursts.

Then, a knock.

I froze.

I stood and shook my limbs. *Get yourself under control Bell.* Taking a few deep breaths I headed to the front door.

There was a knock again just as I peeked through the hole.

"You okay? I was just nearby. Wanted to check on you."

I could smell the coffee and gunpowder on him. He'd been at a scene. Still had the killer's scent on him.

"Yeah," I lied.

He stepped in, his presence filling the room and instantly calming me. His arms wrapped around me, and I melted into them. I hated how safe I felt. Hated how much I needed that safety.

We sat in the dim light of my living room, the city beyond the windows breathing like a beast of its own. Eli poured us a glass of wine, a habit he'd picked up since our third or fourth late-night rendezvous.

"Long day?" He asked, voice low.

I shrugged, taking a sip. "The usual. Teens and their drama. One of my students cried today because her ex-boyfriend liked another girl's story on Instagram."

Eli chuckled. "Tragic."

"It was a national emergency. There were tears. And a TikTok."

He reached over, brushing a curl from my face. "You're good

with them."

"Good enough to lie my way through the day." I leaned into him. "You? Catch any bad guys today?"

His expression dimmed. "Still stuck on the string of stabbings. Same MO. Same clean cuts. No prints, no cameras."

My heart thudded in my chest. I forced my tone to stay light. "Sounds like your killer's got skill."

He looked at me then, searching. "Too much skill. It's like they study every move. Like they're getting better. More confident."

I didn't blink. "You sound impressed."

"I am," he admitted. "But it terrifies me."

"You ever think maybe they're not just a killer? Maybe it's a form of release."

He raised an eyebrow. "Release?"

"Some people scream into pillows. Some hit punching bags. Maybe this one...bleeds others."

He stared at me for a beat too long, then laughed softly. "That might be the most disturbing thing you've said all week."

"You said you were terrified," I reminded him.

He sipped his wine. "I am. Because part of me understands the need for control. That level of precision? On some level I do understand, but there are other outlets besides killing and this guy has killed six people. That's what makes it terrifying."

Later, as he slept beside me, I sat on the edge of the bed, staring at the window. My blade sat on the nightstand, catching the moonlight.

I thought about Connor.

My first.

It wasn't supposed to happen. It was a game. A mistake. One I couldn't take back.

But the feeling it gave me—that high; that release was addictive.

The neighborhood I grew up in taught survival, and sometimes that came with blood. Connor was the first boy who dared to test me, who thought pain made him powerful. He wanted to play rough, wanted me to beg.

But I never begged.

He begged.

After that night, I couldn't stop. The craving etched itself into my bones. It became the pulse under my skin.

I slid under the covers beside Eli again, watching him breathe. His face was peaceful, jaw relaxed, lips slightly parted.

I traced his shoulder with my fingertip.

And now Eli was threatening it.

I could feel the ultimatum looming.

Dinner and Delicious Deception | Eli

The restaurant was one of those quiet, ambient places tucked into the edge of the arts district. Dim lighting, soft jazz humming through the air, linen napkins folded with precision. The kind of spot you only discovered through word of mouth. Bell had picked it. Said she wanted something intimate, something "elevated."

I adjusted the cuff of my shirt as I walked through the door, eyes scanning the room until I saw her.

And just like that, my breath caught.

Isabella sat near the window, the city lights casting a glow over her skin. Her dress was dark green, silky, clinging to her curves like it had been tailored to her. Her hair fell in soft, controlled curls, and the gloss on her lips made me weak at the knees.

I made my way to the table, every step calculated, every breath steadied. Because being around her requires control, especially in public when she looks like that. She made everything harder to manage—my thoughts, my instincts, my goddamn composure.

She looked up and smiled. "Detective Ryder."

"Miss.Carter," I said, smirking as I pulled out my chair. Her brow lifted slightly just enough to register the jab but she let it slide with that same cool, calculating poise I was beginning to know too well.

"Bell." I leaned in and kissed her cheek, letting my lips linger just a second too long. "You look...dangerous tonight."

"Only tonight?"

I chuckled and pulled out my chair. "Fair point."

A waiter arrived with a bottle of red. She'd already chosen it.

"You order for me too?" I asked.

"Would you complain if I did?"

I grinned. "Not if it's good."

The wine was smooth, dry with a hint of spice.

We made small talk while the first course arrived—charcuterie, figs and brie, smoked meats. She asked about my cases, my partner, the latest developments. Always asking. Always probing, even if it was wrapped in casual interest. I studied her face for a second longer than necessary, wondering why she kept circling back to the murders. Most people flinched when I mentioned blood. Bell leaned in.

"You've been really curious about this case," I said, half joking. "Should I be worried you're a crime buff?"

She didn't miss a beat. "Guilty as charged. Podcasts, documentaries, the works. I've always found killers...fascinating."

I raised a brow. "You mean the psychology of them."

She smiled. "Sure. That, too."

I let it go, chuckling. True crime junkie. Figures. "Still nothing on your killer?" she asked, slicing into a piece of Manchego.

"No prints, no DNA. The stab wounds are always the same. Clean. Intentional. The kind of thing someone practiced."

She tilted her head, studying me. "So, it's someone smart."

"Very."

"Sounds like you admire them."

I paused. "I respect the technique. Doesn't mean I want to shake their hand."

She smirked, swirling her wine. "Maybe they want you to."

I leaned forward. "What would you do, Bell? If you were the killer."

She didn't flinch. "I'd keep evolving. Stay clean. Get close to the people chasing me. See if I could make them doubt themselves."

I swallowed a sip of wine and tried not to read too much into it. "You should write novels," I said, lightening the mood.

She smiled. "Ya know I always thought about it. But not true crime but kids books, for middle schoolers." Her eyes beamed as she spoke.

"You want to write books for your students?" I asked picking up on what she was saying.

"Well not specifically for them, but that age group." she said.

"You should do it," I encouraged. She scoffed and giggled awkwardly.

The main course came—herb-crusted lamb for me, salmon glazed with a honey-dill reduction for her. The lamb was tender, crusted with rosemary and cracked black pepper, resting on a bed of roasted root vegetables. She hummed when she tasted her salmon, closed her eyes briefly as if letting it bloom across her tongue.

"That good, huh?" I asked, watching her.

"Better than expected," she said, licking a bit of sauce from the corner of her lip.

My own bite was delicious, but I barely tasted it. My appetite was shifting—my hunger was for something else entirely.

Her fingers grazed the stem of her wine glass, looking at me, teasing me.

The tension between us thickened. Every look, every brush of her knee against mine, was deliberate. By dessert, I was a live wire, ready to burn.

She leaned in close, her voice barely above a whisper. "Come home with me."

Bell's house smelled like vanilla and coconut. What I learned to be her signature scent. Dim lighting, the low hum of music playing from a speaker somewhere, and a faint flicker of candles had my already tense muscles standing at attention. She turned to face me after lighting the last candle and I saw the same hunger I felt in my chest.

She didn't say a word. She just stepped into me and kissed me.

Her mouth claimed mine, teeth grazing my bottom lip as her hands slid under my blazer, pushing it off my shoulders. She kissed me like a dare, slow, but with fire behind it. Her fingers unbuttoned my shirt one button at a time, deliberately brushing her knuckles along my chest.

Then she surprised me by dropping to her knees.

I froze, breath catching in my throat.

Bell looked up at me as she undid my belt, pulling my pants down in one slow motion, her nails dragging lightly against my thighs. It had been a while since we were here, since that one time at the precinct.

She kissed the inside of my thigh. Soft. Open-mouthed. Torture.

"Relax, Detective," she murmured, voice silk and shadows. She moved her hands around to my ass and squeezed.

Her mouth wrapped around me and I gripped the edge of

the wall behind me to stay grounded. She moved slowly at first, letting me feel every bit of her intent. Her tongue tracing maddening patterns. My fingers tangled in her curls, and she moaned around me—intentionally. She was in control, and I let her have it.

By the time I pulled her up, my head was spinning. She smiled and licked her lips.

She climbed on top of me, straddling my hips, hair falling like a curtain around our faces. Her nails dug into my chest, her body grinding against mine.

"You like being in control, don't you?" She whispered.

"I do."

She leaned down, her lips brushing my ear. "So do I."

She rolled her hips, slow and deliberately, making me curse.

When I flipped us over, pinning her beneath me, she gasped, then smiled like I'd passed some kind of test.

Our bodies moved in sync, tension building with every thrust. Her back arched, her hands gripping the sheets, and when she came, it was with a cry that sent a jolt straight through me.

I followed seconds later, collapsing beside her, breath ragged.

Silence wrapped around us.

She turned to me, brushing hair from her face. Her fingers traced along my jaw.

"You ever think you could love someone who scares you?"

The question hit harder than I expected. I watched her lips as she asked it, but it was her eyes that made my chest ache. She was serious. Vulnerable. Or maybe just very good at playing that role.

I tucked a strand of hair behind her ear.

"Yeah," I said quietly. "I think I already do."

She didn't flinch. Didn't smile. Just stared at me like she was memorizing every line of my face.

We laid there in silence for a while, the only sound the hum of her house and our breaths.

"You ever think about quitting?" she asked.

I blinked. "Quitting what?"

"The badge. The chase. All the things that keep you up at night."

I turned my head toward the ceiling. "Naw, I love it."

She traced a lazy circle on my chest. "I think about quitting. Sometimes."

"You don't like teaching?" I asked her.

I felt her shoulders shrug. "No that's not it," she trailed off.

The silence stretched, but it wasn't awkward. It was full—electric, humming with unspoken things. I turned on my side, watching the early morning light edging through the curtains.

Bell shifted closer, her leg slipping over mine. Her skin was warm, her breath even, but her eyes were open. Watching me.

"You thinking again?" she murmured, voice still husky from sleep.

"Always."

She leaned in, her lips brushing mine. This kiss was different. Less fire, more smoke—slow, simmering. But under the surface, something sharper pulsed. Her nails scraped lightly down my chest, then her teeth nipped my bottom lip harder than expected. I groaned, surprised—and turned on.

"Rougher," I murmured.

She bit my neck, hard enough to leave a mark, and straddled me in one fluid motion. Her movements were no longer patient. She rode me with purpose, slamming her hips down until the sound of it filled the room.

I grunted, grabbing her waist, holding on as she took what she wanted. Then I sat up, pressing my chest against hers, and wrapped my hand around her throat. Firm, but careful. Her eyes widened—not with fear, but with hunger.

I tightened slightly, enough to feel her pulse beneath my palm. She moaned into my mouth as I kissed her again.

"You like that?" I growled against her lips.

"Yes," she whispered, her voice ragged.

The control in that moment belonged to both of us, tangled in our shared surrender. And the way she looked at me—dark eyes blazing—made my blood roar.

She leaned in, voice rough in my ear. "You like when I take it from you, don't you?"

I didn't answer.

She slapped my chest once, hard enough to sting.

"Say it."

"Yes," I breathed. "Fuck—yes."

She grinned wickedly, then drove her hips harder. The bed creaked, the headboard slammed against the wall, and I knew my neighbors hated me, but I didn't care. I was too far gone.

When I flipped her over, I pinned both her wrists above her head and fucked her deep, hard, the way she wanted. She gasped, legs locking around me.

"That all you got, Detective?" she challenged.

I growled and gave her everything. Her hand slid around, down my back, and then lower. She grabbed my ass, squeezed hard, then traced along the crease slowly, teasing. I jerked in surprise, but her expression didn't change—she was daring me, pushing boundaries again. My thoughts flickered to the last time. When her fingers dipped lower and the memory made me not protest.

I sucked in a sharp breath and she grinned. "You bring something out of me," I growled.

She rewarded me with a slow, filthy grind that made my vision blur.

We came together in a tangle of force and sweat, our cries muffled by each other's mouths.

She rolled her fingers in a rhythm meant to torture, biting her lip every time I cursed. She took my hands and pinned them above my head, pressing her body harder against mine.

"You've never let anyone do that before, have you?" she whispered.

I shook my head. Couldn't speak.

Her smile was wicked.

She leaned down, licking a line from my collarbone to my jaw before whispering, "Good."

She moved faster then, until the pressure between us snapped. We came together, breathless, tangled in sweat and heat.

This time, when she curled into me, her body was softer.

I didn't close my eyes. I just watched her, wondering how long this could last before everything exploded.

In that moment, I knew: if she was the one I was chasing…

I might never stop running toward her.

She sighed softly and untangled herself from me, sitting up. Her hair was a wild halo around her face, skin glowing in the dim light of early morning.

"Be right back," she murmured, pressing a kiss to my chest before sliding out of bed.

She slipped out of bed and walked toward the adjoining bathroom tucked into the corner of her suite. She disappeared inside with the soft creak of the hinges.

A moment later, I heard the faucet run, then the subtle sound of her peeing, in the quiet room.

The absurd intimacy of it made me smirk.

She always carried herself like this dangerous, controlled storm—but here she was, naked and unguarded, the realness of her settling over me.

I let my head fall back to the pillow, trying to catch my breath again. And maybe figure out what the hell I was going to do about the woman who'd just wrecked my world.

Office Hours | Isabella

The fluorescent lights of my classroom flickered overhead, a buzz in the ceiling syncing up with the scratch of pens against paper and the occasional cough or whispered giggle from the back. It was the period before lunch and most of the students were mentally halfway out the door.

We'd spent the last forty minutes discussing revolutions—how ordinary people could be driven to extraordinary acts of violence when pushed to the edge. I'd posed questions, let them argue over motivations and morals. It fascinated me how easily they labeled historical figures as monsters or heroes.

Now, with five minutes left, I stood at the front of the room and leaned against my desk.

"Alright," I said, my voice cutting through the scattered side conversations. "Quick poll—how many of you think Robespierre was a hero?"

A few hesitant hands rose.

"And how many of you think he was a villain?"

More hands this time.

I nodded slowly, letting the silence settle. "Here's the thing. History isn't written by the good. It's written by the ones who survive. And sometimes, those people do terrible things because they believe it's the only way to make something better."

They were quiet now, eyes fixed on me.

"Your assignment tonight. Pick a revolutionary figure. Someone controversial. Write me two paragraphs defending their actions—and two condemning them. Show me you can see both sides. Even if it makes you uncomfortable."

A murmur passed through the room. I watched them pack up, still thinking.

I liked this class. It let them explore the darker side of humanity. And it let me observe them without suspicion.

I was mid-comment on a student's essay when I heard the knock.

Three raps.

I glanced toward the door.

Eli.

He leaned against the frame in jeans and a dark gray button-up with the sleeves rolled. His badge was tucked away, but I knew it was there. He looked like he didn't belong here and he knew it.

"Miss.Carter," he said, smirking.

I arched an eyebrow. "Detective Ryder. What brings you to my classroom during school hours?"

"Returning the favor," he said smoothly. "Figured since you surprised me at the precinct that one time...I'd repay the visit."

I fought the grin tugging at my lips. I went and closed the door behind him.

"You're lucky this school doesn't do background checks on visitors." He leaned in. "You screening me now?"

"You're interrupting state-funded learning time."

"Then maybe you should punish me."

I narrowed my eyes. He was dangerous when he flirted like this.

I looked up at the clock "I have ten minutes before they return for lunch."

"That's five more than I need." He looked around the room. And glanced back at the door.

I grabbed him by the hand leading him into my empty supply closet, closing and locked the door.

We were inside, door barely latched behind us, when he grabbed my waist and pulled me into him. Our mouths collided in a kiss that left no room for pleasantries. It was all teeth and tongue and heat.

His hand slid up under my blouse, fingers grazing the skin just beneath my bra. He pushed the cups up, exposing my nipples, and rolled one between his fingers until I gasped.

I bit his lip.

"You trying to get me fired, Detective?"

"I figure this repays the lunch visit."

"That was weeks ago," I moaned into his mouth.

"Never let your guard down," he said then pressed my back against the shelves. His hand was already between my thighs, teasing through the fabric of my underwear, fingers dragging along my wet slit.

"You're soaked," he whispered, breath hot against my ear.

"I've been wet since you knocked."

He dropped to his knees and pulled my panties aside, sliding two fingers inside me as he licked slowly, deeply, like he had all the time in the world. I swung one leg over his shoulder, one hand braced against the shelf, the other buried in his hair.

"Fuck, Eli—"

He growled against me, and the vibrations made me moan

louder than I meant to.

He stood, unzipping his pants. My panties were already soaked, clinging to me. He hooked them with two fingers and tugged them down my thighs, letting them fall around my ankles.

His eyes burned into me as he stroked himself once, hard and slow, before pressing the thick head of his dick against my entrance.

"You want it rough?" he murmured.

"Don't hold back," I whispered.

He didn't. He grabbed a fistful of my hair and yanked my head back, forcing my mouth open in a gasp. "That's right," he growled, his breath hot against my ear. "Open that pretty mouth. You gonna beg for it?"

"No," I whispered, smirking through the ache in my scalp.

Spinning me around he slammed into me so hard the shelf rattled, and I nearly lost my balance. He didn't slow down. His thrusts were wild, relentless. Filthy. His other hand landed a sharp smack on my ass, the sound echoing in the cramped space.

"You love it rough," he growled. "You get off on the risk. On knowing you could get caught with my dick buried in you."

"Yes," I hissed. "I'm dripping for it. Keep going. Don't you fucking stop."

He let out a broken groan and slapped my ass again, then grabbed both hips and fucked me so hard my knees buckled. I reached back, nails raking down his thigh, barely able to hold myself up as my orgasm built up like a forest fire.

One hand on my hip, the other tangled in my hair. I braced myself forward against the shelf, arching my back, ass pressed firmly into him, giving him the perfect angle to go deep and hard.

He grabbed both sides of my ass and pulled me back onto his dick, each thrust sharper, rougher. The first thrust stole my breath. The next one made me bite down on my forearm to stay quiet.

"You feel that?" he growled. "That's what happens when you wear that damn skirt."

He slammed into me harder, faster, the sound of our bodies echoing in the tiny space. My exposed breasts bounced with each movement.

He reached around and rubbed my clit in rough, tight circles, the pace brutal and perfect.

I was close. Too close.

"Don't stop," I gasped.

"You're gonna come all over my dick, aren't you?"

"Yes—yes—fuck, Eli!"

I exploded, shaking against the metal shelves, biting down hard to keep from screaming. He didn't stop, fucking me through it, chasing his own release.

He grabbed my throat, pulling me back against him. His thrusts turned punishing, brutal, his hand tightening just enough to steal my breath while the other slammed my hips back onto him. Then I felt it—his fingers trailing lower, slipping between my cheeks.

"Let me see how much you like it," he growled.

Before I could answer, he pressed a slick finger against my tight hole and slowly pushed in. My eyes flew wide.

"Eli—fuck—"

"You gave it to me," he whispered darkly. "Now I'm giving it back."

The stretch burned. The combination of his dick slamming

into me and his finger working deeper made me delirious.

"You like that? You like getting ruined from both ends?"

I nodded, trembling. "Yes—God, yes. Don't stop."

He drove into me harder, finger curling inside me with every thrust, building the pressure faster than I could handle.

"Such a filthy fucking girl," he groaned.

"Take it," he growled. "All of it."

"Yes—fuck—Eli!"

He came with a low, guttural curse, jerking inside me, his release hot and deep. His breath was ragged as he bit down on my shoulder hard enough to leave a mark. I clenched around him, milking every last drop, refusing to let go until I felt him twitch and groan again.

"Fuck," he breathed. "You're gonna be the death of me."

"You'll die happy," I smirked breathlessly.

We stood there for a second, both panting, my forehead pressed against the cold metal.

Then a knock at the door.

"Miss. Carter?"

A student.

We froze.

Eli slapped a hand over my mouth again as I nearly laughed.

He tucked himself away, kissed my shoulder, and zipped up before slipping out, leaving me flushed.

"One moment," I called through the door.

How was I going to get him out of here with the students already back? "You said five minutes," I hissed.

He winked and put his hand on the knob. I hurried to write myself before he swung it open.

"Miss. Carter, it was a pleasure. I look forward to help with your classes. This will be a good partnership."

"Thanks Detective Ryder," I replied stepping out of the supply closet.

He was already gone.

But his scent lingered on my skin—and between my thighs.

And as I sat at my desk, pretending to listen to the discussion, I couldn't stop smiling.

Because this was getting dangerous.

And I loved it.

Unreachable | Isabella

I hadn't seen Eli in days. He was buried beneath late nights, case files, and the kind of exhaustion that didn't leave room for anything soft or warm.

During Video call on Monday night, him in his kitchen, still in jeans and a bulletproof vest, his hair mussed and eyes heavy. He smiled when he saw me, but it didn't reach his eyes.

"You look like shit," I said, sipping wine and curled on my couch in nothing but a long t-shirt.

"You look like a fantasy," he countered. "That I have zero time to indulge in right now."

I pouted. "Not even a five-minute break for phone sex?"

He groaned and dropped his head back against the wall. "Don't tempt me, Bell. I'm running on three hours of sleep."

I set my wine glass aside and shifted the camera lower, letting the hem of my shirt ride up just enough to show a sliver of bare thigh. "I'll keep it quick," I whispered. "Promise."

His eyes darkened immediately. I saw the change in his expression.

"Take it off," he growled. "Now. And do it slow. Make me hard for you like I always am when I think about that filthy mouth and tight little pussy."

His voice had a commanding edge, one that made my core

clench. This wasn't the Eli who sent polite texts or asked how my day was. This was the one who bent me over desks and made me scream into his shoulder.

I stood just far enough from the camera to let him watch as I peeled off the shirt—slowly, teasingly—until I was bare and stretched out across the couch. I spread my legs for him, let him see exactly how wet I was.

"You're gonna touch yourself for me," he ordered, his tone like gravel and heat, already palming himself through his jeans. "But you don't come until I say so. You hear me?"

I nodded.

"Say it," he snapped.

"I won't come until you say so."

"Good girl. Show me what I've been missing."

My fingers slid between my legs, finding my clit, circling it slowly. "I've been thinking about that day in the supply closet," I said. "How rough you were. How deep you got."

He groaned, unzipping his jeans, pulling out his already hard dick. "You were dripping for it. Just like you are now."

I whispered. "You ruined me, Eli."

His hand worked faster as I slipped two fingers inside myself, moaning softly. I added a third and arched my back. "I want your fingers. Your mouth. Your dick. All of it."

"Fuck, Bell—don't stop," he growled. "Spread those legs wider. Let me see that pretty pussy work for it. Rub that clit harder. Moan for me, baby—I want to hear what I do to you."

His voice got darker, more commanding with every word. "You're mine, you know that? No one else gets to see you like this. No one else makes you come like this. Say it."

"I'm yours," I gasped. "Only yours."

"Damn right you are. Now come for me. Come thinking about how I'm gonna bend you over the first flat surface I see and fuck you stupid."

I obeyed, circling faster, panting, my thighs trembling. I was close, aching for it.

"Come for me, baby. Come thinking about how I'm gonna wreck you again the second I get free."

I exploded with a soft cry, biting my lip to muffle the sound, body shaking.

On screen, Eli's face twisted with pleasure as he came, a low groan slipping from his lips.

We both sat in silence for a few seconds, breathless, staring at each other.

"That helped," he said, wiping sweat from his brow.

"Told you it would."

We talked for another ten minutes. He told me about a new lead on the case—another body, this one sloppier than the rest. It had him rattled. I asked questions, careful ones. Nothing too probing. Just enough to make him feel like I cared. And I did. In my own way.

By Wednesday, the calls had dwindled to rushed check-ins. A five-second call while he downed fast food in his car. A text that just said: *Still breathing. Miss you.*

He wasn't gone. But he wasn't here either. And I felt it.

By day four, irritation scratched beneath my skin like a rash. I reread his messages more times than I cared to admit.

I busied myself with work, grading half-assed essays about Stalin and Che Guevara, nodding politely during staff meetings, smirking through conversations I didn't care about.

On Thursday, Alexis noticed. She always did.

Alexis: *You good?*

Isabella: *Peachy*

A few moments later she replied.

Alexis: *I haven't seen you in weeks. You're sulking. Which means this is about a man.*

I raised an eyebrow and pressed the call button.

"Oh so this was so important you needed to call me?" she said as soon as she picked up.

"First of all, I do not sulk," I replied.

"See, you only say that when you're sulking," she shot back.

"Alexis, that makes no sense." I waited for her response but nothing came. I sighed heavily. "I haven't seen Eli all week and I miss him."

"Ahh, pining over your detective lover huh. You need a night out," Alexis said. "Or at least a night off. Come over tonight. Wine, movies, zero men."

I considered it. But I didn't want to, I wanted to go home and sulk. "Fine," I said. "But if you make me watch another 90s romcom, I'm stabbing you."

"Deal."

I showed up to her apartment in leggings and a hoodie, hair in a high puff, bare-faced. Alexis had three bottles of red open and a tray of charcuterie laid out like we were two divorced housewives who hated men but loved cheese.

We started with *Practical Magic*, which she swore wasn't a romcom, just feminist witch drama. Halfway through the second bottle, we were both curled up on the couch, tipsy and ranting.

"Men always want a girl who's mysterious until she actually *is*," Alexis said, pointing her wine glass at the screen. "Then it's too much. Too unpredictable."

"Exactly. They want us dark and sexy but safe."

"I don't want to be safe," she muttered. "I want to be feared."

I smirked. "You're halfway there."

She grinned. "You're the other half."

By the time the credits rolled, she was passed out with her head on my lap, snoring lightly. I stroked her hair absentmindedly, but my mind was already moving elsewhere.

The itch had returned.

Not just the one Eli left behind, but the deeper one—the one that lived in my blood. I could feel it crawling under my skin, whispering in my ear.

Later that night, after I tucked a blanket over Alexis and slipped quietly out of her apartment, I didn't go home.

I went hunting.

Crimson Ready | Isabella

The streets were humid and alive, the city pulsing. Horns honked. Neon bled down the brick walls of late-night bars. The air reeked of booze, cigarette smoke, and desperation. I inhaled it all like oxygen.

I wore red.

Not just any red—*my* red. A deep, dangerous crimson dress that hugged my curves and slit high enough up my thigh to be a promise and a threat. My heels clicked across the pavement as I walked past a group of men outside a bar. Their eyes followed me like I was gravity.

I didn't look back.

I already knew who I wanted.

It started inside a rooftop bar downtown. Classy enough to draw professionals. Loud enough that no one listened. My mark was by the bar. Tan blazer, expensive watch, too much cologne. Alone.

Perfect.

He noticed me the moment I entered. They always did. I brushed past him at the bar, ordered a drink I didn't want, and let my fingers trail just a little too close to his.

"Can I buy your next one?" he asked, voice smooth.

I looked up through my lashes. "Only if you tell me

something interesting."

He smiled like he thought he'd won already. "I'm a venture capitalist."

I almost laughed. "That's not interesting. That's a red flag."

He laughed. He liked that.

Ten minutes later, we were pressed together in a shadowy booth, his hand on my thigh. His name was Jeremy—or maybe Jared. Didn't matter. He talked about himself. I giggled at all the right places. I let him think he was in control.

But I had already decided where and how it would end.

I suggested we leave. He didn't hesitate.

He walked me to his car. An anonymous black coupe parked two blocks away. As soon as we reached it, I turned and kissed him. Hard. Deep. Enough to scramble his brain.

"Wanna come over?" he asked against my mouth.

I bit his bottom lip playfully. "Actually...I have something else in mind."

He followed me like a moth. We cut down an alley between buildings. Dark. Isolated. Exactly what I needed.

"Where are we—"

He didn't finish the sentence.

The familiar weight of the blade was out before he realized.

I shoved him hard against the wall. His back hit brick, knocking the air from his lungs.

"What the f—"

The blade sank into his neck. Quick. Clean. I covered his mouth with my other hand, eyes locked on his.

No screaming. Just shock.

He slid down the wall as I pulled the blade free. Blood painted the bricks. My heart slowed.

There it was.

I rolled my shoulders and exhaled. My blood cooled. The fog in my mind cleared.

I relaxed.

I crouched beside him, watching his final moments like an art critic admiring a masterpiece. Then I stood, wiped the blade, and walked away.

By the time I reached the end of the alley, my dress was still flawless.

My pulse was calm.

I felt *whole*.

Eli was still buried in a case he didn't know he was sleeping with.

But I was back.

And I was *me* again.

Something About Alexis | Isabella

The next morning, I woke up tangled in my sheets, body still humming from the release, from the kill, from being in control again. I rolled over to check my phone. Nothing from Eli. Disappointment pooled in the bottom of my stomach. But there was a text from Alexis.

Alexis: Come over later. I need to tell you something. Bring wine.

That last part softened it—barely. Still, it had a strange energy to it. This had to be serious, no jokes, no shots.

When I got there, she was her usual casual. Hoodie. Bare feet. Hair up. Music playing low from her speaker. But something was off. Her smile didn't quite reach her eyes.

"You okay?" I asked.

"Peachy. Just…feeling weird."

I handed her the bottle of Merlot. "Define weird."

She grabbed two glasses. "Like my past is trying to tap me on the shoulder."

I followed her to the couch and dropped into the cushions beside her. She poured generously, handed me a glass, and then just stared into hers for a beat too long.

"You ever think about how much you'd tell someone if they really pushed?" she asked. "Like, if they asked the wrong question at the right time."

I tilted my head. "Not really. I don't let people push."

She laughed "Of course you don't. You're made of ice and dagger tips. But me? I keep things. Things I probably shouldn't."

Something in her tone made my spine tighten.

"Alexis... did something happen?"

"No. Yes. Kinda." She drained half her glass. "I got a message last night. From someone I haven't talked to in years. Someone I hoped I'd never hear from again."

I studied her, suddenly alert.

"Old flame?"

"Old mistake," she muttered. "And I think he knows where I am now."

My stomach flipped. "You want to tell me who he is?"

"No. Not yet. I just...needed you to know in case I start acting off. Or if I go missing." She said with a half chuckle.

"Alexis. You're scaring me."

She reached out, squeezed my hand. "Don't be scared. Just... keep your eyes open."

I nodded, but my mind was already spinning.

She wasn't carrying baggage. She was dragging it behind her, and it had just started to unzip itself.

Whatever Alexis was hiding, it wasn't harmless.

She poured another glass like nothing had happened and asked me about my kids, about Eli. But I could tell her mind wasn't really with me—it was back with whoever had messaged her. Her knee bounced. Her wine disappeared at an alarming rate. Her smile kept flickering on and off like faulty neon sign.

At one point, she got up to grab something from her bedroom, and I caught a glimpse of her phone screen—open

on a text message. I didn't see the name, just the last message.
We're not finished. You owe me.
My stomach turned.

When she came back, I pretended not to have seen it, but I watched her more closely. The way her eyes darted to the windows. The subtle check of the door lock. The edge of paranoia she tried to hide under a lazy laugh. The way she toyed with the stem of her glass, the way her eyes lingered on the shadows outside her window like she was waiting for them to move.

"Do you trust me, Bell?" she asked suddenly.

The question punched through the silence.

I met her eyes. "Why would I have any reason not to?"

She smiled, but it didn't reach her eyes. "Good. Just…don't stop. No matter what happens."

I watched her carefully.

Something inside her was unraveling, slowly.

"You ever wonder," she said after a long silence, "what would happen if someone pushed you too far? Like…if you snapped. Just once."

I raised a brow. "You thinking about snapping, Alexis?"

She laughed, but it was hollow. "Not yet. But I think I understand now. Why people do it. Why someone might make a permanent choice for a temporary feeling."

My throat tightened. It was personal and it wasn't just fear in her voice.

It was desire.

I knew that tone. I wear it myself.

There was something inside her—something she'd buried—but it was clawing its way out. And whether it was to protect herself or to punish someone, she was closer to crossing the line than she realized.

She was dangerous.

Not yet. But soon.

And when the time came, I knew what I'd see in her eyes.

Not fear.

Fury.

But before things got too heavy, she shifted the mood with a smirk and nudged my leg with hers.

"So," she said, raising a brow. "You and Eli have been getting pretty close huh? It's been what 2 months? Because you're walking around like you've been exorcised."

I smirked. "Girl?" I teased, giving her a playful shove. "I got absolutely wrecked, a lot, and loved every minute of it"

She leaned in, eyes hungry. "Define 'a lot.'"

"He had me bent over the shelves, in the supply closet at school. Next to my students!" I started, swirling the wine in my glass like it was a prop in a confession. "One hand in my hair, the other on my throat. Didn't even give me time to think. Just took."

Alexis fanned herself with a napkin. "Jesus. You're lucky I like you or I'd hate you."

"You would've loved it. He knew exactly what he was doing. I was dripping before he even got my panties off."

She groaned and reached for the wine. "Okay, I need a full scene breakdown."

I grinned and leaned in closer. "He had this hand on my lower back, kept me pressed against the shelf while he fucked me like he wanted to leave bruises. Deep, rough, and filthy. And then—get this—he slipped his finger into my ass."

Alexis gasped, slapping my thigh. "No he didn't!"

"He did," I said, biting back a grin. "Said it was payback."

She blinked. "I swear to God, Bell, you're living in a damn erotic thriller."

"And loving every second of it."

She laughed, loud and full. But beneath the sound, I caught it again—that flicker in her eyes. The kind of look that lingered too long, somewhere between envy and yearning.

Red Smear | Isabella

I hadn't planned on killing again so soon. But the itch didn't care about timing. It came back louder. Sharper. Hungrier.

And I wasn't ready.

It started the same as always. Me slipping into my red dress, the one that felt like armor and bait all at once. Hair perfect. Eyes dark. Smile just sharp enough to cut. I went to a new spot this time. Less polished than my usual haunts. Dirtier. Noisy. Full of transient men and ego.

I found him fast. An easy target. Loud, arrogant, reeking of entitlement. He grabbed the waitress' ass and laughed when she flinched. He didn't see me watching.

We danced around the usual steps. Flirtation. A drink I let him buy. I laughed at his stories, touched his arm, leaned in just enough to make him believe he'd already won. Then I suggested some "fresh air" and led him out the back.

The alley was wet. Smelled like piss and stale beer.

But as I reached into bra for the blade, something flickered behind my ribs.

Not excitement. Not the delicious chill of control.

Doubt.

He turned to face me, breath puffing visible in the cold night air. "You gonna kiss me out here or what?"

I smiled. Slid in close. Ran my hand down his chest.

And froze.

His voice had that same cocky edge Eli used when he teased me. The way he said *mine* when he was inside me, when he had his hand around my throat and his eyes locked on mine. I thought of that day in the supply closet, of the way he'd slammed into me like he couldn't get deep enough. How I'd let him take everything.

And now, here I was and it doesn't feel the same.

Panic flared. My grip on the blade tightened, but my body wouldn't move.

He leaned down, trying to kiss me, and I acted on reflex. The knife came up—too slow, too clumsy. I jabbed instead of doing what I always did: slipping the blade through the artery at the neck, the way I practiced and perfected. And he stumbled back with a grunt.

"What the fuck?!"

He grabbed his side, staggered toward the wall.

"You psycho bitch!"

I lunged, silenced him with a hand to his throat, and finished it. Fast. Dirty. Wrong.

The cut was shallow. His fight wasn't. He scratched me—deep—down my forearm. My breath came in ragged gasps as I drove the blade in a second time, hard, until he went limp.

I wiped the blade with trembling fingers. My hands were slick, not just from blood but sweat. My heart pounded like it wanted out of my chest.

I looked down.

Blood pooled around his boots. I didn't look back. I didn't search the ground. I didn't breathe until I was blocks away and the cold air had numbed my skin. I shoved the blade into my purse and disappeared into the dark.

Back at my house, I dead bolted the door behind me like it could keep guilt out.

I went to the bathroom to undress, and that's when I saw it. My earring was gone.

Panic. I scrambled to my jewelry dish, hoping it had come off earlier, maybe when I was getting ready. But no. Just the one. I ran back to my car, looking under seats, on the floor, everywhere.

One hoop. One missing.

My heart dropped.

I sat on the edge of the tub, hands trembling, breath catching in my throat.

A small, gold hoop. Nothing dramatic. But distinctive. Expensive. Traceable.

I sat on the bathroom floor for nearly an hour, shaking. My red dress clung to me. I stripped it off, tossed it in the tub, and turned on the water.

It stained the porcelain pink.

I scrubbed my arms raw, trying to get his touch off me, the smell of him out of my skin. But it lingered. The scratch on my arm burned the more i rubbed over it.

How stupid can I be.

This was supposed to be my thing. My release. My control. Now it felt like it belonged to someone else.

I crawled into bed with damp hair and shaking fingers, the image of my gold hoop on a dead man's collar burned into my brain. I didn't sleep.

Instead, I stared at the ceiling and imagined scenarios.

Would they find it? Would Eli be the one to pick it up, bag

it, log it into evidence? Would he hold it up to the light and think, *Bell has earrings like this*?

Would he remember the night I wore them for him? When they dangled from my ears while I rode him in his car, too desperate to make it inside?

Or would it get overlooked, cataloged as random debris in a dirty alley?

I didn't know what scared me more—being caught, or being so easily dismissed.

At some point, I rose and poured myself a drink. Whiskey. Neat. The burn steadied me. A false clarity, but I needed it. I sat on my couch, legs folded beneath me, and thought about the girl I was when this all started. Controlled. Precise. A predator in heels.

Now?

I was bleeding. Wounded. Exposed.

I grabbed my phone and opened my gallery. Scrolled past selfies, screenshots, and blurry photos of Eli's bedhead mornings. Then I stopped at the photo I kept hidden in a locked album.

My first.

Connor. Seventeen. Mouth twisted, eyes frozen in fear and betrayal. I'd taken it with trembling hands, a moment after he hit the ground. My kill. My beginning.

I didn't feel proud now.

I felt…unmade.

Maybe it was time to stop.

Maybe it was time to start again.

But either way, I knew this much: I'd lost control.

Suspect | Eli

The alley reeked of rot and steam and something sweet. I screwed up my nose as I crouched next to the body, my gloves sticky with blood as I peeled back the collar of his shirt. And there it was.

A single gold hoop earring, tangled in the fabric near his neck.

"Got something," I called to Spencer. He ducked under the tape and stepped closer, face twisted.

"Another one?"

I nodded. "But it's off. This one's sloppier. Too rushed."

Spencer eyed the blood spatter. He squinted, then smirked. As I stood and pulled out my phone to check the time, the lock screen lit up—a photo of Bell in my hoodie, smiling with her eyes half-lidded, wild curls framing her face. I caught him looking.

"Damn," he said, grinning. "Still your same freak? Because this one's a mess compared to the last guy in the alley. That one had the neck slice, clean and surgical. This? Amateur hour."

He raised a brow. "You and this Bell girl—what, is it official now? Didn't take you for the type to put your girl on your wallpaper. You got that 'sprung' look. All soft eyes and daydreaming at your desk."

I grunted. "We're…spending time together."

"Yeah, and you're about two missed calls away from writing her poetry," he teased.

I ignored him.

"You're smitten, man. It's wild. I never thought I'd see it, but here we are. Eli Ryder, partner and part-time romantic."

"You done?"

He held up his hands in surrender. "I'm just saying. If she ever turns out to be the one leaving bodies in alleys, I'm not betting on you to cuff her. I'm betting on you to cover for her."

I didn't answer. My eyes were on the earring. Expensive. Real gold. Tasteful. Feminine. Not his. The guy was wearing a fake Rolex and a shirt from Target.

Spencer followed my gaze. "Girlfriend's?"

"Maybe. Or the killer's."

He whistled low. "Damn. That'd be a hell of a lead."

Except it wasn't a lead. It was a gut punch.

I'd seen earrings like this before. Not just in passing. Up close. In my hands. Dangling from Bell's ears.

But it couldn't be hers. Could it?

She'd said she had plans the other night. A girls' night. Alexis. Wine. I remembered because I'd wanted to see her and she'd kissed me through the screen and said, *Next time.*

So it couldn't be her.

Still, I bagged the earring myself.

By mid-morning the next day, the lab had a hit—an anonymous tip pointed toward a woman who'd been seen leaving bars with men just like our vics. Young. Curvy. Flirtatious.

Blonde.

Not Bell.

Her name was Sienna Ward. A barmaid, occasional escort,

record for petty theft and drugs. She didn't match the MO exactly, but the media had already run with it—*A female killer, stalking nightlife.*

I was glad for the distraction. It bought me time to breathe.

But deep down, something twisted. Sienna wasn't right. She was too erratic. Too loud and too messy.

Ours—

No. Not ours.

The original ones. The first few. Those were clean. Intentional.

Artistic.

This was noise. But maybe that was good. Maybe it would keep the spotlight off the person I couldn't stop thinking about.

The one whose voice still echoed in my head.

Say it.

I'm yours.

I closed the file and sat back in my chair, heart pounding.

Because I still wasn't sure if I was hunting her—or protecting her.

* * *

Sienna Ward didn't look like a killer.

Her file was a mess of small-time hustles—bar fights, pills, theft, a prostitution charge she pled down to disorderly conduct. But nothing violent. Nothing that screamed what we found in that alley.

Still, she matched the anonymous tip. Blonde. Petite. Curvy. Frequented the nightlife scene. Always cozying up to the kind of men who wound up dead.

Spencer and I found her at a dive bar on the east side, working the late shift. Tight tank top. Shimmering gloss. A laugh that didn't quite reach her eyes.

She saw us coming the moment we stepped in.

"Cops," she muttered to the bartender, sliding off her stool. She didn't run, but she looked like she wanted to. Her smile tightened when we flashed our badges.

"Sienna Ward?" I asked.

"Depends. You arresting me, or buying a drink?"

Spencer chuckled. I didn't.

"We just want to talk."

"That's what they always say."

We brought her in. Not cuffed. She flirted all the way to the precinct—smirking, legs crossed, tongue sharp. But underneath it all? She was nervous.

Interview room. Fluorescent buzz. Two-way mirror.

"You think I killed that guy?" she asked after we showed her the photo.

"We think you were in the area."

"I'm always in the area. You know how many creeps buy me drinks? I flirt, I smile, I get paid. That doesn't mean I slit throats."

"No one said anything about a throat."

She blinked. Just once. But I caught it.

"Lucky guess," she said, too quickly.

Spencer leaned back, arms crossed. "You know what makes people nervous? Saying too much. Too fast."

"You know what makes people defensive? Two guys in cheap suits trying to pin murder on the only woman in the room."

She was clever. Not brilliant. But clever.

We pressed, asked about the earring, the pattern, the nights she couldn't account for. She danced around everything. Denied nothing. Admitted less.

"If I wanted to kill men," she said at one point, "you'd need a much bigger wall to pin bodies to."

Her vibe was off. Too performative. Like she was pretending to be what the media had made her out to be. Femme fatale cosplay.

But we had nothing else.

By the time we cut her loose, it was dark out. Spencer shrugged as she strutted away.

"She's hiding something."

"Yeah. But not what we're looking for."

He looked at me. "You sure?"

No.

Not about Sienna.

All I knew was the earring was still in my desk drawer. And I hadn't told anyone I kept it.

Ghosts | Isabella

I don't think about him often.
    Connor wasn't my first crush or my first boyfriend. He was my first kill. My first slip. The one that shattered the dam inside me and let everything ugly rush through.

I was seventeen. Angry. Raw. Still figuring out how far I could push people before they snapped. Connor was older. College-aged. One of those guys who smiled too much and never took no for an answer.

We met at a party. I was drunk. He offered me a ride. I said yes.

He didn't take me home.

I remember the way his car smelled—cheap cologne and leather seats that stuck to the back of my thighs. I remember him laughing when I told him to stop. I remember fighting, screaming, his hand over my mouth.

And I remember the box cutter in my coat pocket. A habit I picked up from walking alone at night. A precaution.

The blade tore through his neck in one clean motion. Panic and precision in the same breath.

He died making a gurgling sound I still hear in my sleep.

I ran. I didn't tell anyone. I didn't cry. I didn't feel guilt.

Not until the high wore off and the silence crept in. But

even then, part of me felt powerful. Alive. Like something had finally aligned. Like the world had taken its hand off my throat and let me breathe.

I didn't kill again for two years. But after Connor, I wasn't the same. I watched people differently. Weighed them. Measured what I'd do if they crossed the line.

It started small after that. Obsessions. Fantasies. I'd see a man touch a woman without permission and I'd feel the edge of the blade in my hand. Sometimes I followed them. Sometimes I just imagined it. But I was always watching.

Always calculating.

Therapy didn't help. My school counselor told me I had "intensity issues." My mom thought I was acting out because my dad left. No one asked what I really needed. So, I got good at smiling. At blending in. At wearing my skin like armor.

And underneath it, I waited.

College came, and with it, opportunity. New cities. New men. New masks to wear.

I learned how to flirt. How to turn the edge into charm. How to read people fast. I could spot the arrogant ones, the ones who thought no meant "not yet," the ones who touched without permission and laughed when you flinched. I started marking them in my mind.

My second kill was planned. Methodical. I wore gloves. I picked a location with no cameras. I watched him for two weeks before I moved. It wasn't messy like Connor. It was almost beautiful.

Afterward, I didn't feel guilt.

I felt clean.

It was like the chaos in me had a purpose. Like I'd found the valve to let the pressure out.

People think killing is loud. Screaming and blood and dramatic exits.

It's not. It's quiet. Intimate.

It's the look in someone's eyes when they realize they've lost control.

I still think about Connor's eyes sometimes. The way they widened. Not from pain. But from surprise. Like he never thought I had it in me.

They never see me coming.

That's what makes it so easy.

Even now, when I look in the mirror, I see her. That seventeen-year-old girl with a trembling hand and a torn-up coat. She's quieter now, but she hasn't left. She whispers to me in alleys. In elevators.

She whispers.

Remind them.

I do.

Not always with a blade. Sometimes with silence. With sharp words. With power. But the blade is never far.

And sometimes, when the ache in me swells too big to ignore, I wonder if Connor's ghost is still watching.

Because the truth is, I didn't just kill a man that night.

I became one of the monsters I saw on TV. Only smarter. And far, far better at hiding it.

You Ruin Me |Isabella

I hadn't seen Eli in person since the night we both came through the screen. Face Time wasn't the same.

I'd changed clothes five times before I gave up. Settled on silk shorts that were more suggestion than fabric and a black tank with no bra. I was pretending to be casual, but my heart was beating like I was walking into a fight.

Then he knocked.

I opened the door, and there he was.

Bigger. Harder. His fade was fresh, clean along the sides, tight on top. Tired eyes, rough stubble, tension in his shoulders like he hadn't slept right in weeks. His badge was clipped to his hip.

He stared at me for a second too long.

"You look dangerous," he said.

"You look like hell." I let my eyes drop to the front of his jeans. "In a good way. Come in."

He walked past me, and just like that, the air shifted. He was all heat, heavy presence. I tried to focus. Tried to act normal. We put on some movie, something black-and-white and moody.

I curled up next to him, close enough to feel the warmth of his thigh, not touching—yet.

Then I reached for the popcorn. My hand brushed his.

His hand clamped down on mine.

I looked up.

He looked down.

And then he grabbed me by the throat.

The other hand slid under my ass as he pulled me into his lap. Our mouths crashed together, lips hungry, tongues messier than either of us meant. I moaned, fingers in his hair and he bit down on my lip hard enough to make me gasp.

"Missed this mouth," he muttered, dragging my tank up to expose my tits.

"Then stop wasting time."

He stood up with me wrapped around him, carried me straight to the bedroom like I weighed nothing. He tossed me onto the bed, yanked off my shorts and panties in one rough pull, and knelt between my legs.

I didn't have time to say his name.

His mouth was on me—tongue hard and fast, lips sucking like he was trying to make me scream. Which I did. Back arched, fists twisting in the sheets.

No buildup. Just hunger.

He sucked my clit like it was the only thing he wanted in the world. His grip on my thighs would leave bruises. I was already close when he pulled back just long enough to slide his fingers between my cheeks.

One finger pressed into my ass, slick and slow and deep.

"Jesus, Eli—"

"That's what you wanted, right?" He licked up my slit, pushed another finger in, twisting them both. "You open for me already."

I was panting, hips lifting to meet him. When I came, it hit like a punch—sharp, loud, violent.

But he didn't stop.

He worked me through it, tongue relentless, fingers pumping deep until I was shaking.

By the time he stood up, I was wrecked.

He pulled a condom from his wallet, tore it open, and rolled it on with one hand while staring at me.

"You ready?"

He climbed on the bed, dragged me to the edge by my hips, and lined his dick up with my entrance.

"Keep your legs open."

I did. I wanted him.

When he slammed in, I screamed. He didn't go slow. He bottomed out on the first thrust, every inch of him thick and hard, stretching me open until I was shaking again.

"That's it," he growled. "This is my pussy."

He started pounding into me like he was trying to break something. My spine curved off the bed, his name torn from my throat over and over. His hand found my throat and squeezed— my eyes roll back.

"You take it so fucking good," he hissed. "Always so wet for me."

He leaned in, spit on my breast, then licked it up, biting at my nipple until I gasped. His other hand gripped my thigh tight enough to leave marks. I could feel everything. Every inch. Every drag.

"Come," he ordered, rubbing my clit with fast, brutal pressure. "Come on this dick."

I broke. Again. Shaking, breath gone, crying out. He just kept going, fucking me harder, chasing his own release.

When he came, he buried himself deep with a guttural sound,

hips grinding, his whole body flexing as he filled the condom. He collapsed over me; breath ragged against my skin.

We laid there for a minute, panting.

I reached between his thighs, fingers brushing over his balls. He twitched.

"My turn."

He looked at me, dazed. "Shit, Bell…"

I slid down, licked across his abs, stroked his dick back to life while my other hand pressed behind him.

I pushed one finger in, slow, deep, careful. He gasped—loud, sharp.

"Fuck, that's—Jesus—"

I kept going. Worked his prostate while stroking him. He was hard in seconds, hips lifting.

"You ever let anyone touch you like this?"

He shook his head. "Just you."

"Good."

He came again, this time with a broken groan, whole body jerking. I kept my finger inside him, slow, letting him ride it out.

When I crawled back up and kissed him, he looked like he'd been dragged through a war zone.

"What am I going to do with you?" He panted.

She smirked looking up at me.

We laid there, tangled in sweat and heat.

He stroked his hand up and down my arm and noticed the scratch.

"What happened here?" he asked.

I looked up at him-

Then my phone buzzed.

Alexis: *I need you. Come now. Please.*

I sat up quickly.

Eli was watching me. "What is it?"

I read the message aloud.

"You want me to come?"

I hesitated. "No. I gotta see what this is first."

His jaw twitched. But he nodded. "Call me afterwards."

I kissed him, slow. "I will. Stay here."

He watched me get dressed, still catching his breath.

When I walked out the door, a cold knot tightened in my gut.

Whispers In The Dark | Isabella

The scent of Eli still clung to me, sweat, sex and that low hum of satisfaction that came from being touched by someone who knew how. But it all evaporated the second I stepped into the night.

I found myself gripping the steering wheel harder than necessary the entire drive to Alexis's. The streets blurred. My chest tightened with every red light. She lived just outside Uptown, in a modest townhouse she'd decorated like a page out of a vintage catalog. Warm colors, exposed brick, shelves of books and plants.

Her porch light was on. That was new.

I knocked once. She opened the door before I could knock again.

Alexis's eyes were wide, rimmed in pink. She was barefoot, wrapped in a giant hoodie I recognized from a college spring break trip years ago. Her skin was paler than usual, and the tension in her mouth told me everything I needed to know before she said a word.

I stepped inside without waiting for an invitation.

She shut the door, locked it, bolted it. Then turned and leaned her back against it like she needed the solid wood to keep her standing.

"You brought wine?" she asked, voice cracking.

I hadn't. But there was already an open bottle on the table. "I forgot," I said with a shrug. "But it looks like you've got it covered."

I followed her into the living room. The space was dim, only the floor lamp glowing in the corner. Her coffee table was littered with unopened mail, a takeout container, and a folded blanket.

She dropped onto the couch and wordlessly handed me her phone. I stared at the message. A screenshot.

UNKNOWN: *We're not finished. You owe me.*

No name. No number. Just that.

"Ty?" I asked quietly, though I already knew the answer.

She nodded, then reached for the glass of wine she'd clearly been nursing.

"How long's it been since he reached out?"

"Three months. Maybe four. Since the last number he used got blocked."

I sat down beside her, close but not crowding. "You reported this?"

"I called. They told me to 'document and preserve all evidence.' Like I haven't heard that one before."

I sighed, running a hand over my face. "He's escalating."

Alexis let out a sharp laugh. "No shit."

Her voice was hollow, like she was talking through fog. She took a sip of wine, then set the glass down with a clink that sounded louder than it should have.

"I was fine," she said. "I was finally sleeping through the night. And now this shit."

I looked at her, really looked. Alexis had always been vibrant.

Fire in her laugh. Steel in her spine. But right now? She looked like someone had knocked the wind out of her and she hadn't gotten it back.

"He's not here," I said gently. "And you're not alone."

She nodded, but it didn't feel like she heard me.

"You're not staying here tonight."

She glanced at me, blinking. "Bell—"

"No. You're not. You can argue with me when you're thinking straight. Right now you're in panic mode. So I'm not giving you options."

She sighed but didn't fight me. That told me more than her words ever could.

I helped her pack a bag. Toothbrush. Laptop. Hoodie that wasn't two sizes too big. While she was in the bedroom, I looked around. That feeling hadn't left. The one in my gut, telling me this wasn't just a one-time threat.

When she came back, her phone was buzzing again.

We stared at it.

UNKNOWN: *Don't ignore me, Lex. You owe me.*

She didn't touch it. Didn't breathe.

I stepped forward, snatched the phone from the table, and snapped a quick photo of the message with mine.

"Come on," I said. "We're going."

The drive to my house was quiet. I let her sit in the silence. Let her exist without demands.

Once we closed the door, she dropped her bag in the living room. Her eyes trailed the scattering of clothes headed towards the bedroom. She signed heavy.

"Girl, take me home. You got company."

It's only Eli," I said. "Sit down," I demanded.

She relented and sagged onto the couch. I grabbed some

extra blankets and pillows and made up the couch. She didn't argue. Just curled up, small and tense, hugging the throw pillow like it could keep her safe.

I sat on the arm of the couch for a few minutes, watching her eyes flutter closed.

We stayed like that in the dark, both pretending to be calmer than we were.

Alexis curled toward me, her body drawn tight.

"Do you think he's watching me?" she whispered.

"I think he wants you to believe he is."

"Is that a, yes?"

I didn't answer.

After a minute, she said, "I'm scared."

I squeezed her hand under the blanket. "You should be. He's dangerous. But I'm not going to let him get near you. I swear on my life."

She nodded, and for the first time that night, her eyes closed.

But just before her breathing evened out, she whispered something so low I almost missed it.

"Sometimes I think about killing him. Just so he'll stop. Just so I can breathe."

Her voice was flat. Empty. But there was something dangerous sitting underneath it. Something I recognized.

I remembered what it felt like to be cornered. To feel like the only way out was through. I didn't say it out loud, but the thought crept in, quiet and steady: Maybe she was closer to becoming like me than she realized.

Eventually, I stood and walked back to my room, closed the door softly behind me. Eli stirred but didn't talk.

Ty didn't want her back. He wanted control. Wanted her scared. Wanted her power.

And I been done letting assholes like him win.

Loose Threads | Eli

I woke up to the scent of Bell's skin still clinging to the pillow next to me, the faint murmur of her voice in the other room.

Coffee brewed somewhere beyond the closed door. A low hum of conversation, hers and what sounded like Alexis.

My brow furrowed. When did she get here.

The bed was warm. I stayed there for a moment. Then I sat up, groaning a little. I hadn't brought anything with me, no change of clothes, no toothbrush. The jeans from yesterday were wrinkled in a heap on the floor, and my shirt smelled faintly of sweat and sex. I shook it out, trying to release some of the wrinkles, then pulled it on anyway.

That's when I saw it.

A gold earring on the nightstand. Small. Delicate. Half-hidden under a notebook.

It looked a lot like the one we found at the scene the other night.

I stared at it for a moment, then picked it up. Same twist in the metal. Same faint dent near the clasp. It could've been a match. Could've been the other half of the pair.

I slipped it into my pocket.

It could be a coincidence. She bought it from the same place.

Where was the other one? I looked around hurriedly, scanning the dresser, the floor, the shallow jewelry dish. Looking for the pair to relieve this feeling in my gut.

Bell's laugh drifted in, soft and clear. A contrast to the knots building in my chest.

I abandoned the search. By the time I stepped into the living room, Alexis was curled up on the couch, still half-asleep under a blanket, and Bell handed me a travel mug.

"You need to get to work," she asked.

I nodded, gave her a quick kiss on the cheek, and left.

Sienna Ward didn't fit. But that hadn't stopped me from trying to cram her into the box.

She'd lawyer-ed up after her last interview. But I got approval to observe her again, just surveillance this time.

Spencer and I parked outside her usual bar, sipping coffee that tasted like burned cardboard. He was already halfway through his second donut, powdered sugar dusting the front of his jacket like snow.

"You look like shit," he said, glancing at my wrinkled shirt. "Hot night or long one?"

"Both," I muttered, taking a sip of coffee I didn't want.

"You do the walk of shame from your girl's place or did she just throw you out halfway through?"

I shot him a look. He grinned.

"Damn. So it's serious-serious now. Didn't peg you for the spend-the-night type."

"Anyways."

"You're literally wearing the same clothes from yesterday, man. It's a crime of fashion."

I didn't respond. Just watched the bar entrance.

"She's not our girl," I muttered after a while.

Spencer shrugged. "She's got motive. She's got access."

"She doesn't have the control."

He shot me a look. "You mean the precision?"

I nodded slowly. "Exactly."

We watched for another hour. Nothing happened. She worked. Flirted. Collected tips. No one died.

But that pit in my stomach hadn't gone away.

Not since the earring.

Spencer glanced at me sideways. "You keep zoning out like that and I'm gonna start thinking you're in love."

"Whatever man," I said shoving his arm.

"Nah, seriously. Something's chewing on you. You're not this twitchy unless something's off."

I shook my head. "It's nothing solid."

"But it's something, huh?"

I didn't answer. Because it was something.

Not just the earring. Not just the feeling that Sienna was the wrong piece. It was the slow itch that crept up my spine every time I thought too hard about the case.

The pattern didn't match her. The kills were too clean. Too... personal.

Sienna was angry, yeah. But her kind of anger burned quick. Loud. Messy.

These kills weren't messy.

Spencer finished his donut and crumpled the wrapper. "You know, your girlfriend has the right body type, from the video. She fits the description. That woman has you wrapped up tighter than evidence tape."

I shot him another look.

"What? I'm just saying. Does she fit the profile we're working on? I know this last murder doesn't line up, but maybe something happened that made her mess up."

"She's a teacher."

Spencer raised a brow. "And you really think that means anything?"

I didn't respond. Mostly because a small part of me hated how my stomach twisted when he said it.

Bell was clean. Sharp. In control.

And she'd been warm and soft last night, pressed against me like we were something permanent.

I shifted in my seat, pulling the earring from my pocket again. Spencer leaned over. "You carrying jewelry now?"

"Evidence."

His brow furrowed. "You took that from the scene?"

"No. Found it somewhere else. Just…comparing."

He gave me a long look. "Where'd you get it from? Whose is it?"

I didn't say anything. Just watched the bar.

"You better put that into evidence as soon as we get back," he said. "You're going to blow our case." Spencer leaned back, arms crossed. "You know what we need? A break. One real piece that doesn't feel like guesswork."

I nodded slowly.

But all I could think about was that earring. And how close it had been to her bed.

Spencer broke the silence a few minutes later, watching Sienna through the windshield as she lit a cigarette.

"You know what else doesn't sit right? The last murder. It didn't follow the same playbook."

I nodded. "Yeah. The others were tight. Controlled. Almost surgical. This one was…messy."

"Exactly," Spencer said. "It was rushed. Same weapon, Less

control, hesitation. Like whoever did it wasn't thinking—or wasn't used to things going wrong."

Or sending a message, I thought.

Spencer went on. "You think it's a one-off or connected to our case?"

"Have we heard anything back the lab yet?" I asked.

"Nah," he said, "But what do you think?" he asked again not letting it go.

"Don't know yet," I said. "But I don't like the change. If it is the same person, then something rattled them. Or maybe a different person seen the news and trying to slide in their shit unseen."

Spencer tilted his head. "You think it's tied to the specific victim?"

"Maybe. Or maybe they made a mistake and now they're scrambling."

He stared at me for a beat, like he wanted to say more. Then turned his eyes back to the door.

Tangled Patterns | Eli

It was late morning by the time Spencer and I got back to the precinct. I still hadn't changed. The earring burned in my pocket. I hadn't logged it into evidence. Not yet. Couldn't make myself.

The briefing room was empty except for us. We spread everything out—photos, timelines, maps, case notes. Victims one through six. Different backgrounds, different lives, but was it one killer? We just hadn't figured out how they were connected.

Spencer tapped the whiteboard. "Let's start with facts."

"Male," I said. "All six. Similar age range—late thirties to mid-forties."

"Ethnicity varies. Profession too. Blue collar, white collar, service industry."

"Sexual orientation?"

Spencer flipped through a file. "Two were definitely straight. One was bisexual. One… not enough info."

"So nothing there," I muttered. "What about criminal history?"

"One had a sealed domestic case from five years ago. The others, clean."

"Location?"

Spencer opened the laptop, pulled up the map overlay from our analyst. Red dots for the crime scenes, blue for victims' home addresses.

At first glance, it looked like chaos.

"Zoom in on the center cluster," I said.

He did. Three of the crime scenes fell within the same five-mile radius. The fourth was just barely outside it. Their homes were all north of the kill zones.

Spencer leaned in. "That's...tight."

"It's something."

"Same neighborhood?"

"Same side of the city. East corridor. Low foot traffic, minimal camera coverage, few streetlights."

"The killer knows the area."

"Or lives in it."

We went quiet.

I pulled the photos closer and tapped the sixth photo. "This one's the outlier. Rushed. But still within the geography."

Spencer rubbed his chin. "You think they got spooked?"

We went back to the timeline. Dates were random. No pattern. No ritual. But the location... that was the first thread we could tug.

Spencer pointed at a small shaded corner of the map. "You recognize that block?"

I did. Bell lived two streets over.

I didn't say it.

Didn't even let myself feel it.

Spencer kept talking. "Could be someone who works in the area. Delivery driver. Bartender. Janitor. Or..."

"Or someone using a familiar hunting ground," I said.

We built profiles. Mapped foot routes. Checked traffic cams.

None of it gave us anything. Not the same person more than once, the same vehicle, nothing.

Just tighter borders around a predator we still couldn't see.

Eventually, Jason leaned back. "You still thinking this is one killer?"

I hesitated. Then nodded. "Same weapon. That's the link. Cut to the carotid artery. Even the messy one went for the throat."

Spencer tossed a file onto the table. "We need a break. Some thread that ties them together outside the knife."

I stood and walked to the map again. All the dots pulsed under fluorescent light. And somewhere behind my ribs, the earring still burned. I didn't say it, but I already knew: the killer wasn't just operating in that area.

They were rooted there. And one of us already knew them.

Spencer opened another folder and scanned it slowly. "You ever notice how these guys were all creatures of habit?"

I looked up. "How do you mean?"

"I was thinking," Spencer said, flipping through the files again, "what if the victims weren't targeted for their routines—but their locations?"

I raised a brow. "Go on."

"Look at where they were killed. All isolated, low visibility. Easy in and out."

I leaned over the table, studying the map again. "Not following the men. Following the shadows."

"Exactly. She doesn't need to know their habits. She just needs the opportunity." Spencer nodded. "Exactly. Too predictable. Someone could've tracked them without much effort."

"That implies stalking. Planning."

"It always has. But this confirms it wasn't random."

I leaned on the edge of the table, scanning the highlighted sections. "So, the killer picks guys who are easy to pattern. Maybe even watches them for a while."

Spencer pulled up the traffic cam stills. "Look at this. Same silhouette, slim build, caught two blocks from the third scene two nights before the murder."

"Facial ID?"

"Too blurry. But it's something."

I shook my head. I didn't see how a blurry image on a random night was a lead. "We build a timeline off routine instead of just the crime scenes. Start tracking common paths. Whoever's behind this is familiar with predictability."

"Creeping me out how calm they are," Spencer muttered.

"Until they weren't," I reminded him. "Number six."

Spencer turned thoughtful. "Yeah. Something snapped. Either the victim threw her off or something inside them cracked. And because of that, we got evidence."

I took a deep breath. The earring. Was their DNA. I remember the scratch on Bells arm. Will the lab come back with DNA. "Ghost." I said.

"Not a ghost," Spencer quietly. "Someone who knows how not to get caught. Yet."

The silence stretched. I saw Spencer glance at me again, the corner of his mouth twitching.

"Think about it. Small entry wounds. Up close. Fast. No sign of struggle because they didn't see it coming. They didn't *expect* the person standing that close to be a threat."

My pulse ticked up.

Spencer shrugged. "I'm not saying it's your girl. I'm just saying we need to stop assuming the it's Sierra because we both know it's not."

I stayed quiet because the truth was and I had thought about it.

We kept working for another hour, building victim timelines. Identifying their routines. Backtracking their last known steps. All roads circled the same blocks. Same radius. Like someone was drawing the same shape over and over again.

And at the center of it all? A life I was starting to get too close to.

Spencer clapped a hand on my shoulder. "We'll get them. They're slipping. Whoever they are, they're not invisible."

I gave a half-nod then walked to my desk, sat down, and pulled out the earring again.

The metal was warm against my palm. I had to choose.

File it.

Or keep pretending it didn't exist.

I stared at it, my pulse low and steady like I could hold back the flood if I just didn't blink.

Eventually, I closed my hand around it and slipped it back in my pocket.

Not yet.

Not until I was sure.

Fractures | Isabella

Alexis was quiet when I got home. Not asleep. Not crying. Just quiet.

She sat curled on the couch, arms around her knees, eyes locked on the blank television screen. The lamp beside her flickered like it couldn't decide whether to help.

I dropped my keys on the counter gently. "Lex?"

Her voice was steady. "He was in my car."

I froze. "What?"

She didn't look at me. Just uncurled slowly, reached toward the coffee table, and held up a piece of paper.

Lined notebook paper. Torn edges. Folded once.

I walked over, took it carefully, and opened it.

We're not finished. You owe me. Thought you'd want this back.

Inside the folded note was a key—one of those cheap, copy-store ones with her initials scratched into the head. I recognized it. She used to keep it in a magnet box under her bumper.

Alexis finally looked at me. Her eyes were dry. "I lost that key months ago. I thought I hit something and dislodged it."

"How would he—?"

"I don't know. I don't care. He got inside my car, Bell. Into my car." She began to cry.

The air in the room felt smaller. Like every window had been sealed shut and the oxygen was slowly leaking out.

"Did anything else happen?"

"No mess. Nothing missing. But it felt…wrong. Off. Like he'd sat in the seat just to prove he could."

I sat beside her, slowly, carefully. "Did you go inside anywhere? Leave your car unlocked?"

"No. I was at work, parked in the lot, same spot I always use. He knew where I'd be. When I'd be there."

That made my jaw tighten.

Alexis exhaled hard, the breath shuddering through her. "And the worst part is… I felt it. I *knew* something was off before I even opened the door. Like this static in the air. Same way I used to feel around him when he was angry but hadn't said it yet."

My fingers curled into fists. That feeling, God, I remembered it. The chill under the skin. The waiting.

"I hated that," I said softly.

She turned to me. "What?"

"The anticipation. The not-knowing. Feeling like your body recognizes danger before your brain can name it."

Alexis nodded slowly. "Exactly."

I leaned back into the couch, eyes closed for a second. "

It's exactly how I felt in the car with Connor."

She looked at me, eyes widening slightly. "You couldn't have known he was going to do that."

"I knew something was up."

She stared up at me "You never told me that before. Why now?"

I hesitated. "Because I see it in your face. The way you flinch at the door. How you stop breathing when your phone buzzes."

She exhaled shakily. "It's like living in the shadow of someone else's control."

"Exactly."

The room was quiet again, the only sound was the hum of the fridge. "I thought about going to his place tonight," Alexis said.

That made my eyes snap open. "Why?"

"He posted a picture a few weeks ago. I saw the street sign behind him, accidental reflection in a glass door. I reverse-searched the business name. Matched it to the neighborhood. Been narrowing it down every time he posts."

I stared at her.

"I don't know the exact apartment," she added. "But I could find it. If I wanted to."

"And what would you do when you got there?"

She looked away.

"Lex."

"I just wanted to know I *could*," she whispered. "That if I needed to, I could be the one with the power."

My chest ached for her. Because I remembered the first time I had that thought too. The moment I realized that hating someone enough to want them gone didn't make you a monster, it made you a survivor.

"You ever feel like you want to take it back?" she asked suddenly. "The fear. The freezing. The years of letting them live rent-free in your head."

"All the time."

She leaned forward, resting her elbows on her knees. "I wanted to leave something in *his* car. Just to let him know I'm watching too."

"Like what?"

"I don't know. A note. His photo with a knife through it. Something to flip the feeling."

"That would only escalate him."

Her lips pressed into a thin line. "He already escalated."

I watched her for a long moment. The light caught her features in an unfamiliar way—hollowed out, sharp at the edges.

"You're changing," I said softly. "Don't change too much you can't go back."

She didn't argue.

I stood and walked into the kitchen. I filled two glasses of water and stood at the sink longer than I needed to.

When I returned, she was standing now, pacing slightly, chewing at her thumbnail.

"I'm not going to let him win," she said, mostly to herself.

I handed her the glass. "Good."

"But if this keeps going…I don't know who I'll be by the end of it."

I met her eyes. "Someone who survived."

She swallowed. "You just told me don't change too much that I can't change back."

I didn't answer.

Because I'd already crossed that line. And she was inching closer by the day.

She sat again, this time not curled in on herself. Her shoulders were squared, her breath even. Still scared, but sharpening into something else.

"I dreamed last night that I stabbed him," she said quietly.

I didn't move.

"I woke up and didn't feel scared. I felt…calm."

"You're not the only woman who's dreamed about fighting

back," I said. "But you can't act on a dream."

She looked at me. "You ever think about what you'd do differently with Connor?" she asked. Not knowing how far I actually took it with Connor.

"All the time."

"But you don't talk about it."

"No."

"Why?"

I gave a tight nod. "Because I did what I had to do."

Her mouth twitched. Not quite a smile. Not quite a frown. She didn't ask anything else. She didn't need to. She just nodded slowly, like she was turning something over in her head.

Blurred Lines | Eli

That night, I ended up at Bell's again. I told myself it was habit. That I just needed to be near something solid, something warm. But the truth was, I didn't want to be alone with my thoughts. Not after the footage. Not after seeing the woman walk away, knowing something was off, but not having a name for it yet.

Bell didn't ask questions when I showed up. Just let me in, closed the door behind me, and pressed her mouth to mine like she'd been waiting to exhale.

"Where's Alexis?" I muttered into her mouth.

"She said she needed some time. I don't know when she will be back."

I kissed her like I wanted to forget everything—the images of the woman on the footage, the way her hips moved when she walked, and how it all made me feel like I was standing on the edge of something I couldn't control. Bella kissed me back, hot and desperate, her fingers already pulling at my shirt. There was no tenderness. We were both hungry for something we couldn't name.

I had her up against the wall before either of us could think twice. Her hands were already working my pants down, tugging at my zipper. I kissed her harder, deeper, trying to lose myself in the fire of it.

"I need you," I muttered, my breath hot against her neck.

"Then take me," she breathed, her lips brushing my ear, her body already moving against mine.

I didn't hesitate. I tore her pants off, turned her around, and shoved her over the arm of the couch, the fabric creaking beneath us. She gasped, half surprise, half a moan, as I shoved myself into her, not giving her a chance to adjust. I didn't want slow. I wanted raw. I wanted her like she was my only fix.

She moaned when I grabbed her hair, yanked her head back to expose her throat. My hand were on her hips, forcing her to move with me, pushing her into the couch as I fucked her harder, faster, until I was sure she couldn't breathe without me.

"Let me hear you," I growled.

She whimpered, her body clenching around me as I fucked her relentlessly. Every thrust was harder, more brutal, until all that existed was the sound of skin slapping, her ragged breath, and the low creak of the couch. She bit her lip to keep from crying out, but I didn't want silence.

I reached up, pulling her head back again, exposing the line of her neck. "Louder."

She gasped, her voice barely a whisper. "Fuck...Eli."

That was it. That was what I needed. I came hard, deep inside her, with a groan that felt like it was shaking me from the inside out.

We stayed there for a moment, panting, slick with sweat, neither of us saying a word. The only sound was the rapid beating of my heart, still thundering in my chest as I pulled out of her, not wanting to let go. She turned slowly, pulling me with her, leading me to the bedroom.

My mind was still buzzing, the images of the woman in the alley flashing behind my eyes, the earring burning a hole in my pocket on the floor.

Her leg slid between mine as she shifted, her bare thigh brushing against me, already making me stir again. I didn't move—didn't kiss her—just let my hand wander over her hip, down to the curve of her ass. She let out a soft hum, sleepy and satisfied, and I wondered if she had any idea what she was doing to me. I pressed a lazy kiss to her shoulder, breathing her in. She still smelled like Coconut and vanilla, and something about that combination made it hard to think straight.

She lifted her head slightly, brushing her lips across my chest before settling again. "Mmm…round two or sleep?" she murmured, her fingers dragging low across my stomach.

I smirked, but it didn't quite reach my eyes. "Sleep…for now." I couldn't let myself get pulled under again. Not when the dots in my head were starting to connect, whether I wanted them to or not.

Bell shifted against me, her hand tracing lightly along my neck. "You're quiet," she said softly, her voice almost too gentle for what had just happened.

I didn't respond right away. I couldn't. Not when the earring was still in my pocket, still a piece of this puzzle I didn't want to solve.

"Just tired," I muttered, reaching for her hand, squeezing it in mine.

But I wasn't tired. Not really.

Bell's breath was steady now, deep in sleep, but I stayed awake, my mind still buzzing. Every time I closed my eyes, I saw the figure in the footage, moving away. The woman. The shape. The way she'd walked. It made my chest tighten, a feeling I couldn't explain.

I needed answers. I needed clarity. But for now, I had to keep pretending everything was fine, that this wasn't all building up to something I didn't want to face.

And when I finally closed my eyes, it wasn't the quiet I found. It was that voice in my head, a whisper that kept asking, *What if it was her?*

I moved quietly through the room while she slept. Bell stirred when I pulled my hoodie over my head, her eyes fluttering open. She stretched slowly, arching her back like a cat, the sheet slipping down just enough to make it hard to focus.

"Hey" she said, her voice rough with sleep. A lazy smile tugged at her lips, but there was something tight around the edges. "You're sneaking out?"

"Don't say that," I muttered, walking over to sit on the edge of the bed. "Couldn't sleep. Kept thinking about some stuff."

Her smile faltered for half a second, but she caught it quick. "What kind of stuff?"

I shrugged. "The case. We have new footage. It's been messing with my head."

She rolled onto her side, facing me, her fingers ghosting over my knee. "You saw something new?"

"Maybe." I kept my voice even, watching her reaction. She blinked slow, nodded, like she was trying not to show too much interest. "I can't shake it," I added. "The way the woman moves—it's like I've seen it before. You ever feel that? Like your body remembers something before your brain catches up?"

She didn't answer right away. "I mean...maybe," she said finally. "But dreams mess with your head. You're probably just overtired."

I didn't say anything. Her tone was too careful. Like she'd rehearsed it in her sleep.

She leaned in, resting her chin on my shoulder. Her breath was warm against my neck. "You always get weird like this after we sleep together?" she asked, trying to joke—but her tone had a sharp edge under the softness.

I didn't answer and she stilled for a moment. I could feel her weighing something—whether to say it or not. Then her voice dropped to a whisper. "You know this isn't just sex for me, right?"

I looked at her, met her eyes.

"I didn't say it was," I said.

She bit her lip, looked down at her lap, then back at me. "I don't know what this is, but it's not nothing. I feel...something." She let out a shaky laugh. "God, that sounds pathetic."

"It doesn't," I said, and that was the truth. It didn't sound pathetic. It sounded dangerous.

Because I felt something too. I just didn't know if it was real.

Soft and Sharp | Eli

Bell was still asleep when I rolled over, one bare leg tangled around mine, her hair a mess of inky black against my pillowcase. For a second, I just watched her. No badge. No case. No footage looped in my head. Just her—breathing slow, mouth slightly open, like she'd finally let herself rest.

I didn't want to move. Not because I was tired, but because this—her, the quiet, the way her hand stayed clenched in the sheet even in sleep—was the most peace I'd had in days.

Eventually, I slid out of bed. Thankfully, I remembered a bag with clothes this time. I pulled on my sweats and padded into the kitchen. There were dishes in the sink. An empty wine bottle on the counter. The scent of her still everywhere—vanilla, smoke, something darker.

I ran my hand along the edge of the counter, brushing aside a dried coffee ring. Normally, mess like this would bug me. Here? It made the place feel lived-in. Real. Like this wasn't just a temporary escape.

She wandered in a few minutes later, wearing a long silk robe, rubbing sleep from her eyes. "You made coffee?"

"I make damn good coffee," I said, handing her a mug.

She sipped it, narrowed her eyes at me like she didn't want

to admit I was right. "Okay, fine. You're good for something."

She leaned on the counter, legs crossed at the ankle, sipping slow. I watched her like a man who'd never seen quiet before. We didn't say much. There was something about mornings with her that made the rest of the world feel miles away.

"You work today?" she asked eventually, setting her mug down.

"Later, yeah."

She raised a brow. "The dedicated Detective Ryder, skipping work? What's the world coming to?"

"I think it's called burnout," I said. "Or maybe I just like waking up next to you."

She smiled at that—small but real. Then she stepped into my space, pressing a kiss to my chest, resting her head there. "You always talk to women like that, or am I special?"

"You're special," I said.

Her arms looped around my waist, and we stood like that for a while. And for a second, I could see it. Us. A future where I wasn't chasing ghosts and she wasn't made of secrets.

"You ever think about leaving it?" she asked suddenly. "The job?"

Her voice was soft, but it cut through the quiet like a blade.

I hesitated. "You mean quitting?"

She nodded, her cheek still pressed against my chest. "Yeah. Just…letting go of the chase. Letting yourself breathe."

I thought about it. About what it would mean to walk away. I'd never let myself picture that.

"Nah, I love the job," I said. "Never had anything else in my life I was proud of."

She looked up at me, her eyes unreadable. "And if you did? What would you do instead?"

I shrugged. "I don't know. Sleep in. Make coffee. " I said trying to lighten things up.

Her gaze softened. "You ever think about making a like with someone, who that someone might be?"

"Lately I've been feeling like that person is you," I said, looking down at her.

Her body sagged with relief. "Me too," she said. "I've been thinking about quitting for you." she mumbled.

My brows furrowed. "You don't like teaching?"

She paused—just long enough for me to feel it. Then leaned up and kissed me instead of answering.

The kiss was soft, but something about it felt like a redirection. She held it a little too long. Her fingers tightened just slightly against my side. I didn't push.

We spent the morning doing nothing, and somehow that meant everything. She pulled me back to bed. We tangled in the sheets again, slower this time, more careful. Like the first time had burned all the urgency, and now all we had left was need. I didn't think about the badge. Or the earring in evidence. Or the woman in the footage.

I just thought about her. The way her hands shook when she touched my face. The way she whispered my name like it was a promise she hadn't figured out how to keep.

Afterward, she lay curled into me, fingers tracing the faint scar near my ribs.

"You ever wonder what your life would look like if you weren't chasing people?" she asked.

"All the time," I said. "You?"

She nodded. "More than I should." Her voice dropped a little. "Sometimes I think…maybe it's not about what I want to do. Maybe it's about what I can't do anymore."

I turned my head to look at her. "What can't you do?"

She smiled. "Sleep like you do."

It was purposefully vague. And it landed with a quiet thud in my chest.

Later, we sat on the couch, our plates empty between us, legs overlapping, shoulders pressed together. Some crime show played in the background, something half-accurate and full of bullshit. I made a comment about the way the detective held his gun and she laughed, low and warm.

"You really can't turn it off, can you?"

"I try."

"You should try harder," she said, resting her head on my shoulder.

On screen, a woman in a hoodie slipped through an alley. The camera cut to black-and-white surveillance footage, the timestamp flickering in the corner. The resemblance was too close. I felt Bell tense—not much, just a subtle shift, a shallow breath pulled in and held.

She reached for her glass like nothing happened. "They always make the woman guilty in the first act," she said with a small laugh. "And then throw in some twist to make the audience feel clever."

"Yeah," I murmured. "Funny how that works."

She looked at me, her expression open, curious, and just a little too practiced.

And maybe I should have said something. About the case. About how close it was getting. About the way my gut kept whispering her name when I watched that shadow move across the screen. But I didn't.

Because her fingers were laced with mine. Because the house smelled like her. Because for one goddamn moment, I didn't want to ruin it.

I just wanted to keep pretending this was normal. That I could have this and not lose everything else in the process.

And maybe that made me a coward. Or maybe it just made me human.

Kiss me, Kill me | Isabella

I woke with my cheek pressed against warmth. Not the heat of a sunbeam or a fevered dream—but the soft, steady rise of Eli's chest beneath me. His arm was slung around my waist like instinct and our legs were tangled. We'd drifted off that way, skin to skin, his breath ghosting across my neck.

This should feel like peace. The kind of quiet people spend their whole lives chasing. His arm wrapped around me, the steady rhythm of his heartbeat beneath my cheek, the soft hush of early morning light spilling through the blinds. It should lull me into a sense of safety.

But instead, it feels like a trap. Not a physical one. Worse. It's the emotional kind. The kind that creeps in slowly, that sinks its claws into you when you're most vulnerable. That maybe this time, you could be normal. Loved. Held.

My chest is tight, like I've swallowed something too big to keep down—hope, maybe. Or worse, guilt. I'm not built for this softness, this comfort. Every inhale fills me with his scent and the terror that I might want this too much. That I'd trade the blade for this body heat. That the thing inside me, the thing that hunts and feeds, might be losing its grip because of him.

That scares me more than anything. I'm not supposed to feel safe. Safe makes me soft. Safe makes me slow. And slow gets you caught. So I lie here, trying to pretend. Trying to make myself believe that the warmth in my chest is love and not just the warning before the explosion. Every second in his arms, I am not in control. And control? That's the only thing keeping me alive.

I blink up at the ceiling, breath shallow, waiting for the itch to rise. The one that always comes when the calm stretches too long. The one that reminds me I'm not made for stillness. I'm forged in fire. Sharpened in blood.

Eli stirs beside me, his fingers tightening on my hip. "Morning," he rasps, voice like smoke and gravel.

My lips brushed his collarbone. "Morning."

We don't speak after that. Just lay there in the silence. He probably thinks this is intimacy. That I'm letting him in. But I'm not. I'm suffocating.

By midday, the craving claws at me. Not just under my skin, but in my thoughts—persistent and pulsing. I go through the motions: coffee run, lesson plans, a meeting with the school counselor about one of my more volatile students. All while biting the inside of my cheek to keep from losing it. I tell myself it's the stress. The lack of sleep. The hormones. But I know better. I'm overdue.

It's been too long since I've felt that rush, that bloom of power. The last one—messy, hollow—left me unsatisfied. And worse, Eli's hands have started to replace the blade's high. That terrifies me.

So I wait. I watch. And like the universe is listening, the perfect storm appears.

He's the assistant principal at a nearby charter school. I met him at a district training session. Called himself Mr. Reed. Smiled too much. Laughed at his own jokes. The kind of man who flirts with interns and cuts girls off mid-sentence. The kind who hides cruelty under charm. I find his Instagram. His girlfriend looks barely legal.

I follow him after work, hoodie up, keys tucked in my sports bra. I catch him in a parking garage—late, dark, and quiet. The perfect place for monsters. Or monster slayers.

"Mr. Reed?" I call sweetly, stepping from behind a column. He turns, confused. "Do I know—"

I don't let him finish. I'm on him fast, the blade flashing silver under the dim light. I slash—swift, clean—but he dodges, stumbling backward. He's faster than he looks. Panicked now, scrambling for something in his pocket. I surge forward again, jamming the blade into his side before he can even scream.

My hand slips. Blood smears my wrist. His body twists against mine, grabbing at my shoulder, tearing the fabric of my hoodie. I can feel it stretch, rip. I should pull away. I don't. I stab again. This time, the neck. He gurgles, body going limp.

I glance around the alley, heart pounding. I'm breathing too fast and I know better than to rush. But something feels off. That twist in my gut won't let me leave. I scan the shadows, the concrete, his body. Then I see it. Right near his collarbone. A perfect little smear of burgundy, almost black. My lipstick. The one I reapplied in the car, telling myself it was just to look confident.

Stupid. Sloppy. I don't even remember how it happened. Maybe during the struggle, maybe when I leaned in too close. But now it's there. Loud. Like a signature I never meant to leave.

My throat tightens. The high is already gone. I should be in control. Calm, collected. But my hands are trembling, and my body is screaming at me. I take two steps back, eyes still locked on that small and deadly mark. Just a smear of color. It doesn't matter if anyone else sees it. I see it. And I know exactly why I left it.

Because I wasn't focused. I wasn't present. FUCK!

His hands. His voice. The way he mumbles in his sleep. The way he always touches the small of my back like it's second nature.

That softness is becoming a liability.

I force myself to walk, steady and controlled. I look like just another woman headed home, hoodie low, gloves still on. But inside, I'm fraying. I don't breathe right again until I'm home, door locked, lights off.

The hoodie is peeled off and thrown into the bathtub. I rinse the blade—my key—wipe it dry, set it aside. I dig out the lighter fluid from under the sink and toss it in the bathtub. I watch the hoodie burn. The flames twist and consume, but it still doesn't feel like enough. I strip, scrub my hands until the skin is raw. The gloves stayed on, but that doesn't matter. This isn't about blood. This is about what I felt.

Because while I was out there doing what I do best, I was thinking about the man who's undoing me.

I stare at myself in the mirror, steam rising behind me like ghosts. "You're losing control," I whisper.

The thing in me hums.

No, it purrs. *You're falling in love.*

It's nearly midnight when I drive to Eli's. I park down the street, hands gripping the steering wheel like it's the only thing tethering me. I could go home. Pretend I'm tired. Say I had work. But I don't. I need something else tonight. I need to know I can still feel something that isn't soaked in blood.

When he opens the door, he looks surprised. Shirtless.

Sleepy. Beautiful. "Hey," he says, stepping aside.

Mutely, I just step into his arms and press my face to his chest. He holds me like I'm not dangerous.

"Everything okay?"

I nod. Another lie.

He pulls me toward the bed, and I let him.

The Way I Burn | Isabella

He's draped over me.

His arm is heavy across my stomach, grounding and dangerous. I haven't moved. Not really. Just laid here, staring at the ceiling, waiting for my pulse to settle and my thoughts to shut up.

They haven't. Inside, I'm a mess of want and wreckage. I can still feel the blade in my hand. Still see the smear of lipstick I left behind. And worse, I can feel him. Eli. His warmth. His trust. His breath on my skin like it belongs there.

I turn my head slowly, look at him.

He's so peaceful. So unaware of the war happening inches away from his chest.

I should leave. But I don't. Because this is the only place where my hands don't shake.

So instead, I slide closer. My hand slides beneath the covers, resting just above his waistband. Not doing anything. Just… hovering. Feeling the warmth of his skin and the ache building beneath my own.

I should close my eyes. Should force myself to sleep. But I can't. Because I still feel it, the adrenaline, the blood, the release. It's fading, yes, but not gone. Not enough. I'm not sated. I'm not satisfied.

I shift onto my side, press my lips to his shoulder, and let them linger. I inhale slow and deep, grounding myself in the scent of him. Clean and masculine and nothing like death.

He stirs. Not fully awake, but aware enough to turn toward me, his arm wrapping tighter around my waist.

"Bell?" His voice is a sleepy murmur, but his body responds faster. I feel him harden against my thigh and something in me snaps.

I climb on top of him. His eyes flutter open, dazed, confused, then dark with recognition.

"Damn," he whispers, hands finding my hips as I rock once, slow and intentional. "You good?"

No.

I'm not.

But I nod anyway, because I want distraction. I want to get lost in him, in the heat of his body and the weight of his hands, until everything else burns away.

I lean down, my lips barely grazing his, my breath hot against his mouth. "Don't talk," I whisper, my voice rough and thick. "Just fuck me."

He just flips us, takes control.

His mouth moves from my throat to my chest, slow and reverent. Every kiss, every graze of his lips, pulls a sound from me I don't recognize, raw, broken things I didn't mean to give him. It's like he's coaxing confessions straight out of my skin, peeling me open without even trying.

His hands trail lower, dragging heat as they slide between my thighs. The way he touches me is both grounding and devastating. Like he's staking a claim. Like he's daring me to feel safe in something that could ruin me.

And I let him.

I'm not in the alley. I'm not hiding in shadows. I'm in his bed, beneath him, the sheets twisted around my legs like restraints, and for the first time, I'm not running.

But even now, wrapped in warmth, slick with sweat and sin, I can feel the rot blooming under my ribs.

Because my hands are clean tonight, but my heart? My soul?

Filthy. Stained with secrets. Painted in guilt and desire and the unbearable weight of wanting someone this much when I should be slicing my way through the dark.

And still—God, still—I arch into him, begging for more. Not because I need to feel good.

But because I need to feel anything that isn't fear.

When he thrusts into me, it's not slow. It's not sweet. There's no pretense of restraint. It's rough. A collision of skin and need that makes my spine arch and my breath catch. He fills me in a way that feels violent. Like he's trying to fuck the madness out of me and imprint himself in its place.

It's everything I've been trying to outrun, this loss of control; this surrender wrapped in desire. I hate that my body recognizes him like a threat and still begs for more. Every movement is deep, brutal, perfect. No teasing. No mercy. Just him, driving into me with a rhythm that makes my toes curl and my thoughts disintegrate.

I moan into his shoulder, then sink my teeth into his skin— hard. Hard enough to make him hiss through his teeth and thrust even harder. I don't apologize. I want it to bruise. I want him to wake up tomorrow, touch that spot, and remember I was here. That I carved my name into him with more than just a kiss.

I want someone else to see it. I want them to ask. I want him to lie. Or worse—tell the truth.

My nails drag down his back, leaving lines that match the chaos. He groans, low and guttural, like he's the one falling apart. His fingers dig into my hips, possessive, like he can't decide whether to hold me together or rip me wide open. There's desperation in his touch, but something darker too. Something that says he's just as lost in this as I am. He pulls me down harder, hips snapping up with a force that punches the air from my lungs.

One hand slides up my back, under my shirt, splaying across my spine like he needs to feel every inch of me. The other stays on my hip, guiding me, forcing me to take all of him—no pause, no apology. He curses under his breath, hot and ragged against my neck, then bites down just above my collarbone. Not soft. Not romantic. It's a warning. Or maybe a brand.

"Mine," he growls into my skin, voice hoarse and fraying. "You fucking feel that?"

He slams into me, deeper, harder, like he's trying to bury something inside me or drag something out. I don't want love right now.

I want ruin. I want to be torn apart and stitched back together with nothing but sweat and bruises and the memory of what we did here—of how we broke the bed and our better judgment in the same breath.

He grunts, voice rough in my ear. "Fuck, Bell."

I kiss him, hard, swallowing his words.

His mouth crashes into mine, hot, bruising, desperate. I meet him with equal force, fingers sliding into his hair and yanking just hard enough to make him groan. He lifts me easily, hands under my thighs, slamming me back against the mattress without breaking the kiss.

His body presses down, pinning me in place as he thrusts

again—harder, deeper, perfectly unrelenting. My back arches, and he drags his tongue down my neck before biting the curve of my shoulder. My nails rake across his back, leaving welts he doesn't flinch from.

He grabs my wrists, shoves them above my head, and holds them there with one hand. The other drags down my torso, slow, then fast, then buried between my legs again as he drives into me with punishing rhythm. The sound of skin meeting skin fills the room, rough and rhythmic, matched only by the sharp snap of the bed frame against the wall.

"Look at me," he grits out.

When I do, his hips slam into mine with a new purpose. His gaze stays locked on mine—dark, commanding—his jaw tight, breath ragged. He leans in and kisses me again, tongue tangling with mine, swallowing the sounds I can't hold back.

The air hangs heavy with sweat and tension. His hand slides up to my throat, firm and unflinching, applying just enough pressure to steal a breath. My legs lock his waist. I roll my hips, matching every thrust, fast and brutal and addictive. His grip on my wrists tightens as he pounds into me, faster now, rougher, until I'm gasping, writhing, fingers curling into fists above my head.

"Mine," he growls again.

He flips me onto my stomach, pulls my hips up, and plunges back into me so deep I cry out, face pressed to the sheets. His hands grip my waist like he's holding me together, dragging me back into him with each thrust. He sets a new rhythm that leaves bruises, the kind that makes you feel owned.

He leans over me, one hand twisted in my hair, the other flat on the bed beside my head, anchoring himself as his pace turns vicious. My fingers twist in the sheets. My breath stutters. I'm falling apart under him, and he's giving me no room to hide it.

He doesn't pull away right away. Just stays buried in me, breath hot against my spine, both of us slick and trembling. I think it's over.

But then his hand slides lower.

Down my back. Over my ass.

He spreads me open with a rough palm, and I freeze—body taut, breath caught in my throat.

His fingers slide between my cheeks, teasing the tight slick ring of muscle with a single stroke. I let out a shaky exhale, more sound than word, and shift my hips—just enough.

That's all he needs.

"You want this?" he growls into my neck, voice thick and low, his hand still stroking lazy circles that make me twitch under him.

I nod, barely.

His grip tightens in my hair. "Say it."

"Yes," I gasp. "Fuck—yes, I want it."

He groans, then pulls out of me slow and deliberate. I whimper at the emptiness until his fingers slide back in—one at first, stretching me with agonizing patience.

"Relax," he mutters, voice gone hoarse. "Let me in."

I do. Slowly. Inch by inch.

When he pushes in, it's not gentle—but it's careful. And it's all him. One thick, relentless push until he's buried to the hilt, his hands gripping my waist so tight I know I'll feel it tomorrow. I cry out into the pillow. The stretch, the sting, the overwhelming fullness that borders on too much but lands exactly where I need it.

He thrusts slow at first, measured, his hips grinding into mine with a rhythm that steals air from my lungs. Every motion sends lightning through my spine. My hands twist the sheets. My body trembles, stretched and shaking, and he doesn't stop.

"Fuck, you feel that?" he pants, dragging his mouth across my shoulder, sweat dripping onto my back.

"Harder," I whisper.

He does.

He slams into me with a vicious snap of his hips, and I take it all. My cries echo off the walls, mixed with his curses and the filthy sound of skin on skin. It's brutal. It's perfect. It's not just about lust—it's about giving up control, letting him have every inch of me, even the parts I swore no one could ever touch.

He reaches around and rubs between my thighs, fingers rough and fast and cruel. My body tenses. My orgasm crashes into me hard—violent and blinding and absolute. I sob through it, writhing under him as he groans and pumps deep once, twice, then again with a final growl and a shudder that rocks us both.

He collapses over me, breath ragged against my ear, chest heaving. He just holds me from behind, both of us ruined. Spent. Filthy. Shaking. And for once, I don't feel empty after.

I feel owned.

His breathing slows behind me, chest pressed to my back, one arm draped possessively over my waist. I close my eyes, pretending I'm asleep. He presses a kiss to my shoulder—soft, too soft—and then I hear it. Barely a whisper. Like he's afraid of saying it out loud.

"I love you, Bell."

My eyes snap open. He doesn't repeat it. Doesn't ask if I heard. Just holds me tighter, like the words are enough to keep me still.

But they don't.
They detonate. Because now it's not just blood on my hands. It's him.

Bruises Don't Lie | Isabella

It's been a few days since I left Eli's bed with his hands still ghosting over my skin.

We haven't talked about what happened. Haven't dissected the way we unraveled together, limb by limb. He texted. I answered.

But tonight, it's not about him.

It's a wine night. Girl time. One of those evenings Alexis swears we need more of, where the plan is comfort food, big sweats, and enough Pinot to forget we're grown.

Her apartment smells like garlic knots and cocoa butter. The lights are dim, a scented candle flickering on the counter like ambiance can ward off the weight of the week. I'm curled up in her corner chair, glass half full and slippers kicked to the side.

She plops down on the couch across from me, face clean, hair up, over-sized hoodie hiding everything but her eyes—which don't look as relaxed as her body pretends to be.

I swirl my wine and smirk. "Tell me why my student tried to convince me his Chromebook got stolen in the cafeteria…but the dumb ass *live streamed* himself skipping class on it twenty minutes later."

Alexis bursts out laughing, nearly choking on her wine.

"Stop. You're lying."

"I wish I was. And then he got mad—*mad*—when I called home. Said I was 'violating his privacy.'"

She laughs again, head thrown back, eyes crinkling. It's the most relaxed I've seen her in weeks. But it only lasts a breath. Then she pulls her sleeves down over her hands and shifts her legs up beneath her, tucking herself in like she's trying to disappear into the cushions.

I keep going. "Meanwhile, some girl had a full-on meltdown in the hallway because her Air Pods 'caught an attitude' and disconnected mid-TikTok."

"Not the Air Pods being shady!" she says, grinning.

"She told me they've been 'acting different' since the update. Like girl, it's Bluetooth. Not betrayal."

We're both laughing now, leaning into the wine and the ridiculousness of our jobs. Her laugh is real, but it fades too fast. And when she raises her glass again, I notice how carefully she holds it—wrist stiff, arm close to her body, sleeve still low over her hand.

She hasn't pushed her sleeves up once. Not when she reached for the remote. Not when she grabbed her phone. Not even now, when it's warm in the room and the wine's gone to her head.

That's when I start watching between the words.

"Oh my god, you saw Kayla's story?" she says, trying to hide a smirk.

"I did," I reply, leaning in. "She posted a black screen and said, 'I'm not explaining myself to anyone anymore,' and then explained herself for twenty-seven slides."

"Classic Kayla," Alexis laughs, shaking her head.

But when she lifts her wine glass to toast to the chaos, her elbow barely bends. She keeps her arm close to her side, her wrist angled awkwardly. She moves like she's guarding something.

Dark, splotched along the inside of her upper arm, the kind of mark that doesn't happen by accident. The kind of mark someone tries to convince you *was* an accident.

I don't call it out.

Instead, I top off her glass and hand it back like we're still two carefree women swapping dating horror stories and TikTok drama.

"So…" I say casually, taking a slow sip of wine, "Ty's back in the picture?"

She doesn't answer right away. Just focuses too hard on peeling at the label on her bottle. When she finally speaks, it's with a shrug that's too light to be real.

"He's around."

I let the words hang there.

"He's around," I repeat slowly, like I'm testing them for weight. "That's new."

Another shrug. Another fake sip. "It's nothing. He's been… checking in."

"Just checking in?" I ask, eyes locked on hers.

Alexis doesn't blink. "He showed up at my job last week. Brought me lunch. We talked. That's it."

"That's not *nothing*, Lex."

She sighs, and it's the tired kind. "It's not like we're back together or anything. He's just—he's trying."

I raise an eyebrow. "Trying what? To un-terrify you?"

She doesn't respond. Just tugs her sleeve down again and adjusts her position, like the truth's making her skin itch. Her glass is full again, but she's barely drinking now.

"I'm not judging you," I add after a beat, softer. "But I need you to be honest with yourself. You flinch when your phone buzzes. You check your locks twice. And I saw the bruise."

Her jaw tightens. "I told you, that was nothing. I slipped trying to carry laundry—"

I lean forward, setting my wine down.

"Lex," I say, calm, deadly calm, "I know what laundry bruises look like. And that wasn't one."

The room goes quiet. Outside, a car door slams somewhere down the block.

"I'm not scared of him," she says, too quickly.

I nod. "Okay. But do you trust him?"

She doesn't answer. She takes another long sip.

I lean back, watching her over the rim of my glass. "And he still hate when you hang out with me?"

She scoffs, waving it off like a fly. "Ty doesn't hate you. He's just…territorial. You know how guys get."

I don't answer.

Because I do know how guys get. The kind who call you crazy when they've backed you into a corner. The kind who use softness as currency and silence as punishment. The kind who hold your wrist a little too long when they smile.

Speak of the devil.

The front door clicks open.

Alexis freezes for half a second. Most people wouldn't even catch it. But I do.

Ty walks in like he owns the place. Button-down shirt half untucked. Watch flashing. He smiles when he sees us—charming, polite. The kind of smile meant to disarm. His eyes slide from Alexis to me, lingering a beat too long before he kicks off his shoes.

"Evening, ladies." He leans down, pecks Alexis on the cheek. She flinches. It's subtle. But it's there.

I watch him like a wolf watches another predator in its territory.

"You didn't say Bell was coming by," he says, flashing that pretty-boy grin that doesn't reach his eyes.

"Was kind of a last-minute thing," she says quickly. "We're just hanging out."

"Mmm." He walks to the kitchen, grabs a beer from the fridge, cracks it open without asking if we wanted anything. He leans on the counter, watching us with the easy arrogance of a man who thinks he's the smartest person in the room.

He joins us in the living room like it's an interview panel and we're the candidates. Sits beside Alexis, close. One arm slung behind her, fingers just brushing her neck.

"So, Bell." He says my name like it's a dare. "Still molding young minds? Or did the classroom finally break you?"

I smile slowly, deliberately. "Still surviving teenagers and state testing. But thanks for your concern." I lift my glass. "You know, it's always the quiet ones who snap."

He lets out a low chuckle, shaking his head like I'm the punchline to a private joke. "You always had a smart mouth."

"Alexis ever tell you what she was like in college?" he asks, gaze cutting toward her but landing right back on me. "Whole different woman back then. You wouldn't recognize her."

I don't flinch. Just tilt my head. "Yeah? And what changed her?"

He takes a slow pull from the bottle, then smirks. "Life."

He's still smiling, but his eyes are flat. Measuring. Like he's wondering how far he can push before I push back. He gets off the couch to walk past me, and this time, his hand drops briefly to my shoulder. His thumb presses, not hard—but *firm*. Like a warning. Like a message.

His voice is soft, low, just for me.

"Some people don't know how to stay in their lane."

The moment Ty's footsteps disappear down the hall, the air changes.

Alexis doesn't look at me. Just stares into her wine like she's trying to drink herself into a different timeline.

I sit forward, elbows on my knees, eyes on her—not soft. Not kind. Calculating. Because I know what she's doing. I've done it.

"You gonna tell me what that was?" I ask.

Her jaw clenches. "Don't."

"You're flinching. You're drinking like it's medicine. You haven't touched your phone since he walked in."

"I said don't."

I nod, sit back. "Right. Because if you don't talk about it, it's not real."

She exhales sharply. "You don't get it."

"No?" I lean forward again, voice low and cold. "I've seen that look in the mirror. I know what it feels like to lie to yourself so well you start believing him. To cover bruises with makeup and blame it on furniture. To let someone wrap their fingers around your voice until you forget how to scream."

Her hand tightens around the stem of her wine glass so hard I hear it creak.

"I'm not scared," she mutters.

I stare at her. "You should be."

Her eyes snap to mine.

"Because it's not gonna stop," I continue. "The squeeze on your wrist turns into a shove. The shove becomes a grab.

Then it's a slap. Then it's waking up on the bathroom floor wondering what you did to deserve it."

Tears threaten, but she blinks them away.

"He's not like that anymore," she whispers. But it's weak. Like she's repeating a line someone else rehearsed for her.

"You don't have to live like this," I say, same words as before—but this time, sharper. Heavier.

She sets the wine glass down. Her hands are trembling.

"What would you do?" she asks, voice shaking. "If it were you?"

I meet her eyes. No flinching.

"I'd kill him."

She doesn't argue. Doesn't tell me I'm crazy. She just sits there, staring at the spot where Ty stood minutes ago like she can still feel his presence staining the air.

Just grabs the wine bottle and refills her glass like she's trying to drown the conversation before it takes root. Her hands are shaking, but her face is blank now—blank in that way that says everything inside is screaming.

I watch her swallow a mouthful too fast, wincing as it burns its way down. She's unraveling. Like a bomb learning patience.

She laughs then. Just once. It's short and brittle, like glass cracking under pressure.

"You're really something, Bell," she says, staring straight ahead.

"Yeah," I murmur. "I get that a lot."

She sets the bottle down a little too hard. Wine sloshes over the rim. She doesn't notice. Or maybe she doesn't care.

The bruise on her arm is exposed. Neither of us says anything about it.

She reaches for the remote, changes the subject with a fake

smile and a too-cheerful tone.

"Let's put on something dumb. I can't handle any more serious tonight."

Let her pretend.

The Tell | Eli

The alley reeked like most crime scenes did—piss, beer, and fresh regret. I crouched beside the body, my fingers tightening around the latex gloves as I examined the wound. One clean cut to the throat. Same as the others. But this time, something was wrong.

The guy was younger than the others. A little more put together. His wallet was still in his back pocket, and his watch, an Omega I couldn't afford on a detective's salary, glinted under the weak light like a final middle finger. This wasn't a robbery. Never was.

"Got something weird here," Spencer muttered behind me. My partner's voice had that tone—tight, skeptical, and annoyed.

"Define weird," I said without looking up.

"Lipstick," he said, squatting next to me. He pulled out a small evidence bag, sealed tight around a white swab tinged with burgundy.

I frowned. "Lipstick?"

"Yeah, smudged on his collarbone. Not on the lips. Not kiss-marked either. Just…a smear. Forensics will run it once we get it back to the lab."

My gaze locked on the red blotch, barely noticeable on his

skin if you weren't looking. The blood made it hard to tell at first, but now that I knew what to look for, it stood out like a warning flare.

"You think it was part of the struggle?"

Spencer shook his head. "Nah. It was intentional. Too clean. Like it was left there on purpose."

I stood up slowly, wiping sweat from my brow. My mind was already racing, trying to connect dots I didn't want to admit existed.

"What's his name?" I asked.

Jason flipped open his notebook. "Reed. Jeremy Reed. Worked as an assistant principal over at Jefferson Charter. Just transferred in last semester."

The name hit me like a gut punch.

Jefferson.

Bell's school.

I kept my face still, but inside, something began to unravel.

"You good?" Spencer asked, catching the slip in my expression.

"Yeah. Just tired," I muttered, turning away before he could press further.

We canvassed the area, but as usual, no witnesses. No cameras. Whoever was doing this knew how to vanish. But this kill felt different. Sloppy in a way that wasn't physical—sloppy in motive. This wasn't just about the kill anymore. It felt personal.

Spencer and I split up after the scene, and I told him I was heading back to the station. Instead, I drove toward Jefferson.

The building was quiet in the late afternoon haze, kids long gone, the parking lot half-empty. I just watched from across the street, engine idling. My fingers tapped restlessly on the steering wheel, my thoughts louder than the talk radio buzz in the background.

I wasn't here for work. I was here for her.

Bell talked about work often—usually in sarcastic rants filled with dramatic flair and side commentary. The annoying principal, the TikTok-obsessed ninth graders, even a lunchroom food fight that made her laugh for days. Reed's name had never come up. Maybe that wasn't strange. Maybe he was just background noise. But something about the omission felt deliberate. Like a corner left untouched in an otherwise chaotic room.

So why did I feel like she knew him?

I parked a few blocks away and walked into a nearby coffee shop. The barista didn't blink when I asked for the school newsletter. I told her I was a parent. She handed it over with a smile. I took it to the corner table and started flipping pages.

Fourth page in, there it was. A training seminar photo. Teachers lined up in that overly posed, forced smile kind of way. Bell, front row, hand on her hip. To her left was...

Jeremy Reed. Grinning.

I stared at the photo for longer than I needed to. Bell's smile wasn't her real one. It was that professional tight-lip thing she used at mandatory functions. The same one she used on me the first time we met. Reed's hand hovered near her waist, fingers too close for comfort. She hadn't leaned in.

My gut twisted.

I pulled out my phone and opened the photo album. Scrolled past the random memes she sent me, the blurry shots of her in over-sized hoodies, selfies in my bed. And then I stopped.

A photo of her on my lap. Her hair a mess, lips glossy, eyes half-lidded. She'd worn a dark burgundy shade that night. I remember it vividly because it had been all over my neck the next morning.

I zoomed in on the photo until her lips filled the screen, and that deep burgundy shade came into sharp focus. It looked just like the one from the crime scene—rich, dark, and too damn specific to ignore. A slow, sinking weight settled in my chest as realization clawed its way in.

That lipstick wasn't common. She once told me it was custom-mixed at some bougie-ass beauty counter in the mall. Said it made her feel like a villains in a romance novel.

My hands shook slightly as I shoved the phone back in my pocket. I could explain it away. Coincidence. Maybe someone else wore the same shade. Maybe she wasn't involved. Maybe.

But then why had she never mentioned Reed? Why was there a smear of her lipstick on his goddamn body?

Back in the car, I pulled out the evidence bag with the earring. I hadn't filed it yet.

I opened my glove compartment. Pulled out the earring I found under the seat two nights ago. It must have slipped off Bell during one of our late-night drives. I held them side by side.

They were identical—same make, same elegant twist in the design, and even the same small dent near the clasp that I hadn't noticed until now. My breath caught in my throat, and a quiet, visceral curse slipped out as the truth pressed in closer than I was ready for.

I dropped both earrings into the center console, slammed it shut, and sat in the driver's seat with the engine still off.

What the hell was I supposed to do with this?

Bell was smart. Calculated. But this? This didn't feel like her usual control. Something about it was off—like whoever left those clues wasn't thinking straight. Maybe it wasn't her. Or maybe she was slipping. Either way, it was the first time the killer had left room for doubt—and that alone was enough to mess with my head.

Spencer was right. The latest kills had been messy. Hesitant. It lacked the surgical precision the others had. Like someone had been too focused on something else.

I closed my eyes, pinched the bridge of my nose, and leaned back against the seat.

Maybe she wasn't the killer. Maybe someone was trying to frame her. Maybe someone stole her lipstick. Maybe she had a twin I didn't know about.

Shit! I slammed my hands down.

I didn't believe it, and I hated that I couldn't even lie to myself.

Bell had secrets. I knew that. She wasn't a girl who wore her past on her sleeve. But I never thought she'd bury it in someone else's throat.

I turned on the car and pulled away from the curb. I didn't go back to the precinct. I didn't go home.

I went to her house.

She opened the door in a silk robe, hair twisted up, skin glowing in a way that made me ache and recoil at the same time. Her smile faded the second she saw my face.

"What happened?" she asked, stepping aside to let me in.

I walked past her and stood in the middle of her living room, trying to decide if I was here as a detective or as her man.

"I need to ask you something," I said finally, turning to face her.

She nodded slowly, tension heavy in the air. "Okay. Ask."

"Do you know a Jeremy Reed?"

Her eyes flickered. Just once. Quick. But I caught it.

"He works at Jefferson. We've met—briefly—during a training seminar. Why?"

"Did you keep in touch?"

She tilted her head. "Not really. He used to hover a little too close during meetings. Said a few things that rubbed me the wrong way, so I kept my distance."

I watched her. "When did you last see him?"

"A few weeks ago. Maybe more. Why are you asking about him?"

"Because he's dead, Bell."

Her face didn't change. Not at first. Then her lips parted slightly, and her hand tightened around the knot of her robe.

"What?"

"Found in an alley behind a parking garage. Same M.O. as the others. Clean cut. Except this one was messy. Sloppy. And there was lipstick. Same color you wore last week."

"That lipstick," she said slowly, crossing her arms, "you think it looks like mine?"

I met her eyes. "It's not exactly a shade I see around often."

"So what?" she asked. "You think I was there, that it was me?"

I hesitated. "I don't know what to think, Bell. But too many things are starting to circle back to you—and not in ways I can ignore."

"You think I killed someone and then what? Came back and curled up in your arms?"

I stepped forward. "Don't do that. Don't make this about trust."

"It is about trust," she snapped. "Because if you think I'm capable of that, then what the hell are we doing, Eli?"

I reached into my jacket pocket and pulled out the earring. I didn't say anything. Just held it up.

Her eyes widened for half a second.

"Where did you get that?"

"From in your room. And we found its twin at the one of the scenes."

She stared at the earring, then looked at me.

"What are you going to do?"

That was the question. That had been the question since the moment I realized I was falling for her.

I pocketed the earring.

"I don't know yet."

She exhaled, slow and shaky. Then she walked over to me, stopping just inches away.

"If I told you I had secrets—ones that would make you hate me—would you still stay?"

My jaw clenched. "Depends on how many bodies are attached to those secrets."

She almost laughed. Almost.

"Then I guess we'll find out."

I looked at her, trying to make sense of what was real and what was an act. There was fear in her eyes. Maybe guilt. But no sign of panic. No plea for me to believe her.

For the first time, I couldn't tell if I was talking to the woman I'd fallen for—or to the prime suspect in my case.

I didn't know which answer scared me more.

Sloppy Seconds | Isabella

It had been seventeen days since Eli stopped looking at me like I was someone he could trust. Seventeen days since his touches turned polite, his questions tighter, and his goodbye kisses stopped landing anywhere near my mouth. The space between us just echoed.

He still came over sometimes. Still slept beside me like a man trying to remember what intimacy used to feel like without bleeding. But his arms didn't wrap around me anymore. His gaze didn't linger. He hadn't said "I love you" in nearly three weeks. And when he did look at me, it was with something distant in his eyes—like he was trying to figure out what version of me had made it home that night.

I knew what that meant. He was watching me. Not like a lover. Like a man building a case.

Honestly. I couldn't even blame him.

I hadn't killed anyone since Reed. That mess was still haunting me. I could feel it in the way my phone vibrated a little too loud during staff meetings. The way I caught myself double-checking door locks, the edges of mirrors, the soles of my boots. I'd left something behind—I didn't know what, exactly—but it was enough to change the air between us.

"You look like hell," Alexis said as she dropped her bag onto the table, sliding into the seat across from me like she'd been waiting for the right dramatic moment. "Did Eli finally figure out you're the emotionally unavailable one in the relationship?"

I didn't bother. My appetite had been missing for days, but I picked at my lunch just to keep her from making a scene.

"Not even a comeback?" she asked, raising both eyebrows. "Okay, now I'm actually worried."

"I'm just tired," I said, stabbing a tomato with more force than necessary.

"You've been tired for two weeks. That's not tired, that's withered."

I rolled my eyes, but she was watching me with that too-perceptive look—the one she wore when she was studying people she didn't trust.

"Seriously," she added, lowering her voice. "You're quieter. Weirdly so. And you haven't threatened to choke a student since Tuesday. That's three whole days of abnormally chill Bell. I miss violent Bell."

"She's still here," I muttered flatly.

"Good," Alexis replied, picking up a french fry. "Because I might need her."

I looked up slowly.

"What's going on?"

She hesitated, just for a second. "Things with Ty are worse."

I pushed my tray aside, giving her my full attention now.

"He showed up outside my place again," she said, her voice tight. "I changed the locks last week, so he couldn't let himself in this time. But he didn't even try. He just stood there outside of my window. Didn't knock. Didn't text. Just...watched."

My grip tightened on the edge of the table.

"He's not touching me," she continued. "Yet. But it's like he wants me to know he could. And that I can't prove anything."

I was already building scenarios in my head. Exits, shadows, timing. Which alley. Which method.

"Say something," Alexis said.

"What do you want me to say?" I asked, my voice lower than before.

"I don't know. Something. Anything that doesn't sound like you're planning his funeral in your head."

I blinked slowly. "What if I am?"

Alexis leaned back, intrigued. "You're serious, aren't you?"

I didn't answer.

"You know, if I didn't already think you were scary," she added, "this would definitely be the moment I started."

That night, Eli didn't come over.

No text. No check-in. Not even a ghost of a message like he used to send when things were good. I sat on my couch in the dark, legs curled under me, staring at the TV but not watching it. Some show with perfect people and perfect problems played in the background while my own thoughts chewed through me like acid.

I didn't regret killing Reed.

But I regretted being messy.

I regretted letting my emotions drive the blade instead of my plan. That wasn't the kind of killer I wanted to be. That was the kind of killer who got caught.

Alexis showed up uninvited the next evening with two bottles of wine, a pack of Reese's, and a bag of greasy Thai food like she was staging a breakup intervention.

"I brought carbs, sarcasm, and a bottle of Merlot so cheap it might be poison," she announced as she nudged the door shut with her hip.

"I don't drink on Wednesdays," I said, deadpan.

She paused, blinking. "Bell, it's Friday."

I stared at her for a second, then nodded. "That tracks."

We didn't talk much at first. Just sat on my couch, our legs tangled in opposite directions, sharing Pad Thai and watching some reality show neither of us cared about.

About halfway through the second episode, Alexis spoke without looking at me.

"Do you ever wish you could just erase someone?"

My fingers froze around the wine glass. "What do you mean?"

She shrugged. "Not kill, exactly. Just…remove them. Like Ctrl-alt-delete but for people. Wipe them out of your life. Like they never existed."

I didn't speak.

She turned her head toward me, voice quieter. "Ty's getting worse. I'm just waiting for the part where he stops pretending."

I looked at her profile, the shape of her jaw, the hard edge in her expression she was trying to pass off as indifferent. But she was cracking. And I was beginning to understand why.

"If someone like that just…disappeared," she said. "I don't think I'd be sad about it."

I set my wine glass down carefully. "Would you be able to live with it?"

She looked at me then. Really looked.

"Are you asking hypothetically?" she said.

I tilted my head. "I'm asking as someone who's tired of pretending monsters are only in stories."

Alexis didn't laugh. She just said, "I think I already know how to live with it."

Everything shifted.

The next morning, I woke up with the decision already made. One more.

That night, Alexis crashed on my couch after we drained half a bottle of wine and picked through the remains of the pad Thai. She didn't press me. But the quiet between us felt heavier than the buzz from the alcohol.

She fell asleep in her hoodie, curled into the corner like she was guarding something.

I didn't sleep at all.

I lay on the floor, eyes open, tracking the lines in the ceiling. My mind kept circling the same memory, the same name I'd buried under years of excuses and half-healed trauma. I thought I'd let him go. I thought I'd moved on.

I used to think Connor was the worst of them. That ending him would be enough. That if I took out the hand that hurt me, the rest of the body would rot.

But he wasn't the root, he was just the first branch that snapped under pressure.

The next morning, Alexis texted me as soon as she left.

"We didn't talk about it."

I stared at the screen, thumb hovering over the reply bubble. I wasn't sure if she meant Ty. Or me. Or the thing we were both circling but hadn't dared to name.

Eventually, I typed:

"There wasn't anything to say."

She replied almost instantly.

"That's the problem."

A minute later, a third text came through.

"Call me when you're ready. Or tell me where to be."

This time, I didn't answer.

Not because I didn't want to. But because I already knew I

would and she already knew I meant it.

Too Quiet | Eli

Three weeks.

That's how long it had been since I found the second earring. Since Bell stopped making excuses that sounded like anything but. Since I started keeping my distance, and she stopped pretending to mind.

I hadn't been over in nearly a week. The last time I came by, she kissed my cheek like a stranger and didn't ask where I'd been. We'd stopped pretending things were normal. At least, I had.

She still sent check-in texts, but they were shorter. Emptier. I didn't push. I didn't ask. We were holding space like a cold war—two people circling the same silence, waiting to see who would speak first and who would bleed.

Some nights I couldn't sleep. Not because I was afraid of what I'd find—because I was afraid I already knew.

I'd sit at my kitchen table long after the lights were off, trying to remember the sound of her laugh when it wasn't hiding something. I'd replay the way she used to say my name—low, teasing, full of heat—and wonder if it had ever been real. If any of it had.

I still loved her. That was the worst part.

Not past tense. Not maybe. I loved her. Fully. Stupidly.

But every time I looked at the evidence, the gaps narrowed. The pattern sharpened. And the person I cared about more than anything was standing at the center of it.

This wasn't just a case anymore.

It was a war between my gut and my heart—and no matter who won, I already knew I was going to lose.

I'd been digging for weeks.

Jeremy Reed's file was thin. Assistant principal. Transferred schools twice. No disciplinary history. But there was a weird footnote—his name had once come up in a mentorship roster I recognized. Not because of Reed, but because of someone else listed alongside him.

Connor Maddox.

Connor Maddox.

He was already dead. Murdered under circumstances that had never made sense. The case had gone cold quickly, like someone wanted it forgotten.

It wasn't technically part of my current caseload, but something about it snagged. I double-checked the document, then pulled Connor's employment record.

He'd worked in the same district as Reed—same time frame, same professional development sessions. No known infractions, but something about it felt off.

And once I started looking into him, things started to line up in ways that had nothing to do with coincidence.

I checked archived staff photos and induction rosters from almost ten years back. Both Connor and Reed had been part of a new teacher mentorship initiative—fresh hires, barely credentialed, attending the kind of seminars where everyone wore too-bright smiles and khakis that didn't fit right. Connor looked young—maybe twenty-four. Reed was probably a few years older. Both had that same smug look I'd seen on men who thought consequences were optional.

That training program took place almost a decade ago. I didn't think about Bell at first—there was no reason to. I was focused on Reed, on Connor, on what tied them together. But something about the way their names kept circling the same institutions made me wonder who else had been caught in the orbit. I remembered Bella once mentioning she grew up in that area. Nothing specific—just an offhand comment about school lunches and cheap lockers.

That's when I asked Spencer to pull student records from the district. Just to rule it out.

Connor looked young in the photos—mid-twenties, maybe— but it was clear he wasn't some high school boyfriend. He was already in a position of authority back then. A grown man in a room full of students, praised by the system, given a microphone and a pedestal. Old enough to know better.

I didn't know how Reed fit into that story—if he was complicit or just nearby—but the connection was there. Same program. Same district. Same ugly orbit.

I asked Spencer to pull old student records from Bella's district. It wasn't easy—half of them were still on paper, boxed up in storage rooms no one had touched in years. He called in a favor with a clerk he used to date and got us access to a back room that reeked of mildew. We spent an hour digging through stacks of dusty boxes before Jason slid a yearbook across the table, his brow furrowed.

"Didn't you say that guy, Connor, used to teach around here?"

Page forty-two. There she was. Fifteen years old, unsmiling, eyes sharp. Two pages later, a photo from a mentorship assembly. Connor at the podium. Jeremy Reed standing beside him. Both labeled as guest speakers from the district initiative.

Bell had been in that crowd. She'd been in their world. A student surrounded by men the school had praised—men they'd told her to trust.

Not colleagues. It was intimate. Institutional. Unavoidable.

And maybe that was enough to scar her. Maybe it was enough to make her bleed them dry.

Spencer didn't know what I was working on, but he'd stopped asking.

"You gonna start looking like a person again or should I start writing your eulogy?" he asked over a cold sandwich and the sound of a flickering overhead light.

"I'm almost there," I muttered.

"Almost where?"

I didn't answer. He didn't press.

I hadn't put Bell's name in any report. Not officially. But I had a private notebook Where I started mapping it all. Hoover. Connor. Reed. All different methods. All close to Bell in ways that were too precise to be coincidence.

And then there was the lipstick.

I'd taken a swab sample—quietly—to a friend in the lab. She didn't ask many questions. Just raised an eyebrow when I asked her to match the pigment base.

The DNA from the previous scene came back, but there was no matches in the system to compare it to.

The swab came back two days later. "High-end. Custom blend. Something from a boutique line. Not drugstore. Not mass-produced."

Bell had once told me that exact shade made her feel like a

villain in a romance novel.

I couldn't forget that.

That night, I drove to her place.

I didn't text. Didn't call ahead. Just pulled up, shut off the engine, and sat there staring at the porch light she always left on. The one that used to feel like a welcome.

She opened the door before I knocked. Just stood there, one hand on the frame, eyebrows raised like she'd been expecting me. She wore a tank top and pajama shorts, barefoot, skin glowing in that way that always made my pulse stumble.

"You look like hell," she said, voice soft but unflinching.

"I came to talk."

She stepped aside. "Then talk."

I walked in, ignoring the familiar ache that tightened in my chest. The living room smelled like her shampoo. A candle flickered on the counter.

She stood across from me, arms crossed loosely like she wasn't sure if she needed to guard herself or let me in.

I didn't sit. "Jeremy Reed. Connor Maddox. Michael Hoover."

Her jaw tensed, but she didn't speak.

"They're connected," I said. "I know you were a student in the same district. In the room during those mentorship events."

Still, she said nothing. Bell walked past me slowly, deliberately. She poured a glass of water at the sink, took a long sip, and set it down. Then she turned.

"And what exactly do you think I've done, Eli?"

I met her gaze. "I think you're not finished."

She walked toward me then—steady, smooth, eyes locked to mine. And when she stopped just inches away, I felt the burn rise behind my ribs.

"I'm tired," she said. "Of pretending not to notice the way you've changed. The questions you don't ask. The way you lock your drawer now. I see it, Eli. I see *everything*."

"Tell me the truth," I whispered.

She reached up, dragged her fingers along my jaw, slow and deliberate. "Do you really want it?"

"Yes."

"Even if it ruins this?" I didn't answer. Didn't need to. Because she kissed me.

It wasn't soft. It wasn't sweet.

Her mouth against mine, her hands threading into my shirt like she was tearing it open and holding it together all at once. I backed her into the wall and felt her exhale into my mouth like she wanted to devour every hesitation.

She bit my lip. Hard. Enough to make me grunt and grip her tighter. Her legs wrapped around me without invitation, and I lifted her with instinct, driven by something primal.

Her nails dragging across my back. There would be marks. I slammed her hips against the wall, swallowed her gasp, and kissed her harder.

She pulled back just enough to look me dead in the eye. "Still want the truth?"

"Tell me."

She dragged her fingers through my hair, pulled my mouth back to hers, and said against my lips, "You already know it."

We didn't make it to the couch.

She clawed my shirt off before I had her tank top over her head. Her body arched into mine, every inch of her daring me to keep going.

Her nails dug into my shoulders as I spun her around, pressing her chest to the wall like a suspect under arrest. I didn't speak. There was nothing to say—just breath, just movement, just punishment and permission tangled together.

Her breath hitched when my hand slid lower, dragging across the curve of her ass before gripping it—hard. She arched and moaned, and I knew she wasn't expecting gentleness.

I slapped it once. Then again. Her hips pressed back like she wanted more.

"Is this what you want?" I growled, my fingers spreading her cheeks to tease along the cleft. She gasped, half turning to look at me over her shoulder—eyes blazing, lips parted.

"Don't stop," she whispered.

I slid lower, thumb brushing down until she flinched. She was already shaking, and I hadn't even started. One hand held her steady. The other explored every inch she didn't offer to anyone else.

The way she whimpered, the way her thighs trembled, the way she whispered my name like a curse—it was addictive. And I wanted to ruin her for anyone else.

When I finally pushed into her, it was rough. My hand never left her ass, fingers digging in with every thrust, every groan, every filthy promise she dragged out of me.

We didn't stop until the world blurred.

We didn't stop until her knees buckled and I had to catch her.

We didn't stop until the only sound left in the room was the echo of everything we didn't say out loud.

Between The Line and The Lie | Eli

She was still asleep when I sat up on her couch, neck stiff from passing out. The blanket she'd tossed over me was already slipping to the floor. Sunlight filtered through her half-shut blinds, catching on the empty glass on the table, the discarded clothes, the mess we'd made.

I should've left hours ago.

She stirred, turning over in the bed just across from me. Her voice was low, groggy. "You always this creepy in the morning?"

I ran a hand over my face. "Didn't want to wake you."

"You already did." She sat up, blanket slipping down her back, hair wild. "You always brood this loud?"

I stood, trying to shake off the weight crawling across my skin. "You want coffee?"

She gave me a look. "You gonna make it?"

"Fair point."

She slipped out of bed in a tank top and boy shorts, grabbed a hoodie off the back of a chair, and pulled it on.

"You gonna pace all morning or actually say what's on your mind?" she asked, voice casual but eyes sharp.

I didn't answer.

She stepped into the kitchen, grabbed two mugs, and poured

the last of the coffee. No offer. Just a second cup placed silently in front of me.

"Black," she said.

"You remember that?"

"I remember a lot of things I probably shouldn't."

I leaned on the counter, hands wrapped around the mug I wasn't drinking from. "Bell… they're connecting the victims."

She didn't look up. "They would."

"They're all over the board, but someone's starting to see the overlap."

"You?"

She finally met my eyes. "So what are you going to do? Arrest me? Was last night part of your investigation?"

I winced.

She planted herself across from me, the counter now the only thing between us.

"I didn't lie to you," she said. "You just didn't ask the right questions."

"Then let me ask now," I said. "Did you kill them?"

"Yes," she said, steady and unapologetic.

The word landed between us like a lit match in a room soaked with gasoline. I didn't breathe. Just stood there, fully aware that the line I'd been pretending didn't exist had now been crossed—and she hadn't flinched doing it.

"I know about Connor," I said, watching her reaction. "At first, I didn't think he fit the pattern. But then I pulled the file. It was closed—labeled a code case, no leads."

Bell didn't flinch. Just crossed her arms, leaning back like she'd been waiting for this.

"That was a long time ago," she said quietly. She exhaled slowly, eyes fixed on the floor. "He was the first person who made me feel powerless. I didn't want to be that girl again."

I didn't press. I already knew I didn't want to hear the details.

"Is that what this is to you?

She shrugged. "To the ones no one else holds accountable? Yeah. You could say that."

"And the others?" I pressed. "You think it was justice?"

"I think justice is a luxury."

I stared at her, unsure if I wanted her to keep talking or stop before she shattered whatever image I was still clinging to.

She didn't look away. "Connor was a mistake. He was a loss of control. I didn't know what I was doing."

My throat tightened. "And the others?"

Her jaw flexed. "They weren't him. But they were close enough. Different names. Same games. You know the type."

I did know the type—men who walked through life with power no one gave them but everyone let them keep.

"They don't stop," she said, quieter now. "Not unless someone makes them."

There was no plea in her voice. No spin. Just plain truth.

That's what made it dangerous. I looked at her—really looked—and the unease in my chest turned into something messier. Heavier. Because for the first time, I wasn't sure if I was more afraid of what she'd done…or of how easy it was to see *why*.

"I haven't put your name in any report," I said. "Not yet."

She tilted her head. "You planning to?"

"I don't know."

She stepped closer, the tension shifting from cold to resigned.

"How long do I have?" she asked, voice calm.

I blinked. "What?"

"Before you turn me in," she clarified. "Before the cuffs, the questions, the paperwork."

"You think I've already made that decision?"

She shrugged and looked at me.

Everything in me twisted. "You're not some random name on a file. You're not just a suspect."

"No," she agreed, quiet now. "I'm something worse. I'm someone you care about." She crossed her arms, her tone gentler. "So why haven't you written my name down yet?"

"Because I don't know if I'm doing my job… or trying to protect you," I said, the words rougher than I meant.

"Which is it?"

"I don't know," I said again, and this time it felt like a confession. "I keep thinking I can separate it—you and the case. But I can't. I think about you more than the evidence."

She blinked once, slowly. "That's not fair."

"It's not," I agreed. "I'm not supposed to want you. I'm supposed to stop you."

"And yet you're still here."

"I am."

Her voice softened, just enough to sting. "Then say it, Eli. Say what this is."

I looked at her for a long time, and for a moment, I thought I could. But all that came out was, "I don't know. I don't know if I chose you…or if I just lost the part of me that knew how to say no."

She just stared back, arms folded like she was holding herself together. Then, quiet and steady, she said it.

"I love you."

There was no performance in it. No trembling voice. Just the kind of truth that doesn't come with expectations—only consequences.

My pulse roared in my ears. I wanted to stay. God, I wanted to wrap my arms around her and forget every badge, every rule, every line I'd ever sworn to follow. But staying meant choosing her—choosing this—and I wasn't sure I could live with what that meant.

I stepped back.

She didn't stop me. She just stood there, like she'd already prepared for this part.

"I need time," I said, the words barely making it past the tension in my chest. "I need to think."

Bell nodded once, slow and certain. "You won't get a better answer tomorrow than the one you already feel right now."

Maybe she was right. Maybe I already knew.

But I still grabbed my keys. I still walked out the door.

I didn't look back.

Everything Is Quiet Expect The Cracks | Isabella

The house was too quiet. No texts. No knocks. No Eli. I hadn't touched my phone since he walked out. It buzzed a few times—group chat pings, a missed call from Alexis, My phone buzzed again—group chat ping, missed call from Alexis. I didn't answer. Whatever she needed could wait.

I focused on the sound of the faucet dripping in the kitchen. The way the sun bled through the blinds. I hated the silence when it came with this much space to think.

"I love you." I'd said it like I didn't expect anything back. And he'd left like he didn't have anything left to give.

I didn't cry. I just sat still long enough to feel it curl in my chest, heavy and sharp.

That's when Alexis showed up. She didn't knock. She had a key and too many opinions.

"Your face looks like shit," she said by way of greeting, dropping a takeout bag on the counter.

"Good to see you too."

"Figured you hadn't eaten." She opened the fridge, frowned at the emptiness, then shut it like it had personally offended her.

I didn't say anything. She finally stopped moving, turned, and really looked at me. "Okay. What happened?"

I hesitated.

"Don't lie," she added. "You only sit like that when something's broken or bleeding."

"He left."

Her eyes narrowed. "Eli?"

I nodded.

"Why?"

"Because I told him the truth."

"He really walked out on you?"

I nodded.

"Why? What'd you say?"

I looked at her, really looked at her. "I told him what I did."

"Okay..." she said slowly, still not connecting it. "Like, what kind of *did*?"

"I told him about the bodies. About what I've done."

Alexis stared. Blinked once. "Wait. You're serious."

"Yeah."

"You told a cop you've killed people?"

"I told *Eli*. There's a difference."

She let out a low whistle, hands braced on the back of the chair. "Shit."

"He didn't arrest me. But he left."

Alexis sat back, lips pressed into a line. "How long has this been going on?"

I didn't look away. "A while."

She just nodded once, slow and thoughtful, like something in her finally clicked.

"Okay," she said, voice quieter now. "Good to know."

"He had evidence, he has evidence. So I told the truth."

She didn't argue with that. Just stared at the floor for a long moment.

Then she whispered "Ty's been texting me."

That snapped my attention. "Why?"

"Same reason he always does. To pretend like he didn't ruin everything and I'm the crazy one."

I sat up straighter. "You didn't respond, right?"

"No."

"Alexis—"

"I said no, B." Her voice was tight. "I'm trying not to be that girl anymore."

I wanted to believe her. I did.

But her hands were clenched in her lap. Her nails were digging into her skin.

"He's doing that thing again," she muttered. "Circling. Liking old photos. Messaging my friends. I blocked him, but he always finds a new number. A new way in."

"You want me to handle it?"

She looked up, lips pressed into a thin line. "Would you?"

"Say the word."

Her jaw worked, like she was chewing on something sharp. "No. Not yet."

"Not yet?" I gave her a look. "What are you thinking?"

Alexis stood, pacing to the window. "I'm thinking…he's getting careless. He's too used to no consequences. If I wait much longer, he's gonna put his hands on someone else. Or worse."

"Lex," I warned.

She turned back around. Something darkened in her expression.

"I want him gone," she said. "But not sloppy. Not reckless. I want it done right.

I raised an eyebrow. "You're really thinking about this."

"I'm *past* thinking," she said. "I just need help making sure no one ever finds him."

The weight of her words landed hard.

I tilted my head. "So what does that look like?"

"I used to dream about running into him," she said. "In public. Somewhere I couldn't pretend not to see him."

I stayed quiet.

"In those dreams, I always froze. Couldn't move. Couldn't speak. Just watched him walk away again."

Her fingers tightened on the edge of the counter.

"I don't want to freeze anymore."

I nodded once, slowly. "Let me know if you need backup."

She didn't smile. Just pushed the takeout box toward me.

"Eat something before you start spiraling again," she said, already heading for the door.

I watched her go. She hadn't asked for help.

Saved or Signed Death Warrant | Isabella

The second night without Eli felt louder than the first. The quiet had weight now, pressing in behind my ribs, curling around my lungs like a vice. No footsteps in the hallway. No voice in the next room. No low hum of him making coffee that he always forgot to offer me.

I sat on the edge of the bed, staring at the wall like it might offer clarity. It didn't. The same peeling paint. The same crooked frame I'd meant to fix. The same damn silence.

He hadn't called.

He hadn't texted.

And I hadn't stopped checking. I told him the truth. And he walked away.

That should've been the end of it. But if it were, I wouldn't have spent two hours last night pacing my apartment trying to decide whether I should bleach everything or burn it to the ground.

He said he hadn't written my name in a report.

But that didn't mean no one else had.

The earring, the lipstick. Connor's file. If Eli had seen the pattern, someone else could too. I just didn't know how far behind they were. Or how much time I had left.

There was a black SUV parked across the street.

It hadn't been there yesterday.

I clocked it through the window while pretending to scroll through my phone. Tinted windows. Clean frame. Government tags. No one got out. No one went in. Just parked.

It could've been nothing. But I didn't believe in coincidences anymore.

I moved from the window, grabbed the burner tucked inside the box of old files beneath my bathroom sink.

I stared at the lock screen for a full minute.

If I ran now, I might be okay. I had cash. I had fake IDs. I had contacts from a life I hadn't touched in years. The network was still there. If I reached out, someone would answer.

But I didn't move.

Because running would prove him right—that I was exactly what he feared.

Or worse—that I didn't care what he thought at all. And I wasn't sure I wanted to disappear if it meant losing the last person who ever saw the real me and didn't flinch—at least, not right away.

I tucked the burner back in the sink.

Instead, I cleaned. Not because the apartment was dirty—but because it gave my hands something to do while my mind threatened to self-destruct.

I wiped down surfaces that were already spotless. I re-bagged trash that didn't need bagging. I opened drawers and re-folded things I hadn't worn in months.

And then I found the box.

It was tucked behind a false panel in my closet. I hadn't opened it in over a year.

Inside were remnants. Tokens. Things I told myself weren't

trophies even though they clearly were. A key card. A watch. A receipt with blood on the edge that had dried into rust-colored lace. Nothing traceable. Nothing I thought would ever come back to haunt me.

I stared at it all, breathing steady.

I could get rid of it.

Toss it. Burn it. Leave no trace.

But instead—I cataloged it.

Every piece. Every detail. I laid it out and took photos, stored them on an encrypted drive I'd hidden in the smoke alarm.

I didn't know if I was building a safety net or a confession. Maybe both.

There was a knock at the door.

I froze.

Three quick taps. Not the casual kind. Not the neighbor kind.

I moved toward the door without making a sound and checked the peephole.

Plainclothes. Male. Clean cut. Thirty-something. Too stiff to be a neighbor, too polite-looking to be a threat. The kind of man who showed a badge without ever flashing it.

I didn't answer.

I waited until he left a card wedged in the door frame.

Then I picked it up with gloved fingers and memorized the name.

Detective K. Morris. Homicide Division.

He didn't knock on anyone else's door. Just mine. I shut the door and double-locked it.

My phone buzzed a minute later.

Alexis: *You okay?*

I stared at the screen.

She hadn't checked in since the Ty conversation. She'd left with too many questions and not enough promises. I thought she'd need space to process what I'd told her.

But maybe she wasn't just processing.

Maybe she was paying attention in a way I hadn't expected—watching me, measuring my unraveling in real time.

I stared at her text for a second before replying: *I'm fine.*

She didn't hesitate: *Liar.*

I didn't respond.

The next morning, when I opened my door, there was another card waiting. Not from the detective this time. No badge, no title—just three numbers written in clean, familiar handwriting.

The next morning, another knock.

Alexis, leaning in the doorway with that look on her face. The one that meant things were already in motion.

"I thought about it," she said.

"About what?"

"What you told me. And what I want to do about Ty."

Whatever line we thought we'd drawn between what was survivable and what wasn't—

It was gone now.

And we were both standing on the other side of it.

I stepped aside, letting the door click shut behind her. Alexis hovered, restless, wound tight, like something had been simmering under her skin since the last time we spoke.

"You weren't wrong," she said finally. "About him. About Ty."

I stayed quiet.

"He's still trying," she continued. "Still circling. The calls, the likes, the mutuals he pretends to forget he shares with me. He's pushing again, testing how far he can go without me snapping."

"And are you?" I asked. "Snapping?"

"I don't want to be afraid of him," she said. "And I'm not. Not really. But I'm tired. Of looking over my shoulder. Of pretending it's fine that he gets to walk free and I have to pretend nothing ever happened."

I exhaled slowly. "So what now?"

She met my gaze head-on.

"Now I stop pretending." There was a sharp edge that hadn't been there before.

"And me?" I asked. "Why come back?"

"I needed to know you meant it," she said. "That you weren't bluffing. That what you told me was real."

I didn't flinch. "It was."

She nodded once, more to herself than to me.

"Good," she said. "Because if I'm going to do this, I need someone who understands what comes after."

I swallowed hard, pulse ticking up.

"You want help?"

"I want cover," she said. "Guidance. The kind you don't get from a Google search."

I could already feel the floor shifting beneath us—this invisible threshold we kept pretending we hadn't already crossed.

And now, she was asking me to open the door wider.

To make room.

To teach her.

"I'm not a mentor," I said finally.

"No," Alexis replied. "But you survived it. And I'm not trying to be you. I ran before. Started over. I'm not doing that again."

I looked at her, really looked at her and saw it.

That flicker I'd once carried. The one that came right before the first time I stopped being afraid.

And just like that, it was done.

I didn't know if I'd just saved her. Or signed her death warrant.

But either way she wasn't alone anymore.

The Thin Blue Line | Eli

The evidence board was starting to look like a threat. Connor's case file was back up. Hoover too. Reed's photo hovered in the center like a warning sign I kept ignoring. Everything was starting to converge, and the more I stared at it, the more it looked like a noose.

Jason leaned against the opposite desk, flipping through a file with casual attention I couldn't afford. His tie was loose. His coffee was cold. But his eyes were sharp, locked on a witness statement that had been flagged for follow-up.

"Still no match on the lipstick print," he said, finally breaking the silence. "We got a partial off the glass at the last scene, but nothing useful. No hits in CODIS either."

"Whoever this is? They're careful. It's like they don't leave anything behind unless they want us to find it."

That was the part that kept me up at night.

Because I'd seen that kind of precision before. Up close.

Spencer kept flipping. "You think it's the same person across the board?"

I shrugged. "Feels like it."

"It's a stretch," he said. "Different M.O.s, different weapons. Time gaps. Unless they're adapting…"

"They are," I said, too fast. "It's evolving. Getting smarter."

Jason raised an eyebrow. "You say that like you know them."

I forced a smirk. "Feels that way when you're knee-deep in the files for too long."

He didn't question it. Just tossed the folder on the desk. "Still can't believe they reopened Connor's case. That thing was ice cold."

"Not anymore," I muttered.

Spencer tapped a new report into the system, humming low under his breath. Something about the way he moved, like this was routine, made me want to tear the whole board down.

Because it wasn't routine. Not to me.

I opened my desk drawer and stared at the notebook inside.

The one with Bell's name nowhere on the cover—but everywhere on the pages.

Notes. Patterns. Photographs I shouldn't have taken. Quotes from witnesses I never submitted. And one photo I hadn't been able to delete—her earring, the second one.

I hadn't logged it.

I told myself it wasn't enough to mean anything. That it was circumstantial. That I was protecting the investigation by keeping it off the record until I was sure.

But that was a lie. I was protecting her.

Jason stepped out to grab another round of coffee, and I snapped the drawer shut before he could see.

The guilt was a dull knife that twisted every time someone said "victim" like it didn't mean anything personal. Like I wasn't sleeping with the common thread tying all of them together.

I moved to the board, stared at Reed's timeline again.

The night he died, Bell had an alibi—sort of.

She said she was home. Said she was alone. And I hadn't

verified it.

Because I hadn't wanted to.

It was easier to pretend I hadn't seen the flash of recognition in her eyes when I showed her Reed's file. Or the way her voice dropped when she asked if the killer was targeting "men like him."

She already knew the answer.

And I'd known what that meant. Even then.

There was a knock on the office door.

Jason popped his head back in. "Morris just called. Wants to compare notes."

I went still. "Detective Morris?"

"Yeah. Cold case guy. Got assigned to one of the reopened. Thinks he's onto something with the lipstick. Said it matches a pattern from Connor's case—wants to know if we've seen it before."

"I'll take that call," I said, voice steady even as my stomach dropped. "Send him through when he's ready."

Spencer gave me a look, but didn't press. "Sure thing."

As soon as he left, I sat down and opened the drawer again.

The earring was still there. The photo of it, tucked into the pages of my notebook like it belonged there.

If Morris saw it, he'd ask questions.

If Spencer saw it, he'd make assumptions.

II stared at it for a long moment, fingers hovering just above the edge. Then I closed the drawer again. Locked it.

The phone rang ten minutes later.

I let it buzz twice before picking up. "Ryder."

"Detective Eli Ryder?" The voice on the other end was clipped. "This is Detective K. Morris out of the Cold Case Division. Appreciate you making time."

"No problem," I lied.

"I've been reviewing files tied to three unsolved from your precinct—Hoover, Marcus Ingram, and one you've got open now. Reed. I'm seeing some consistencies. Subtle ones."

"What kind of consistencies?"

"Signature-style placements. Minor things. Clean kills, no evidence, precise throat wounds. It's subtle."

I exhaled slowly. "You think it's the same person."

"I think it could be. And if it is, they've evolved. Hoover's scene was brutal but chaotic. Reed's was calculated."

Calculated.

That word echoed in my skull like a gavel drop.

Morris kept talking. "I ran the lipstick. Nothing in CODIS, but I matched it to a discontinued boutique brand. Color's called 'Bloodmoon,' limited release from a niche Black-owned line out of New Orleans."

"Anything else?" I managed.

"Actually, yeah," he said. "There's a pattern I found in the Connor file—close-range kills, no defensive wounds, same type of blade injury. The clean-up job was surgical. Whoever did it didn't panic…they planned."

I gripped the phone tighter. "You sure?"

"Clear as day once. Don't know what it means yet, but it felt intentional."

Goddamn it.

"Thanks for the update," I said, my voice too even. "Let me know if anything else surfaces."

Morris paused. "We'll be pulling copies of your open reports. Anything sensitive I should know about?"

I hesitated. "Nothing outside of what's already in the file."

He grunted. "Alright. I'll follow protocol."

Click.

The moment the line went dead, I sank into my chair, elbows on knees, forehead in my palms.

He was getting closer.

The earring. The notebook. My silence. If this unraveled, I wouldn't just go down as a cop who missed it. I'd be the one who tampered with evidence.

There was a folder sitting on my desk labeled **REED – 04/04**.

I opened it, flipping past the official statements, past the photographs, past the reports. All of it was clinical, cold. Processed by people who hadn't sat in Bell's living room with her breath still on their skin.

People who didn't know her laugh. Or her fury. Or her reasons.

My phone buzzed again. Spencer this time.

Grab lunch?

I pushed from my desk ready for another distraction

I did. And that made me dangerous—not to her, but to the case.

Because somewhere between the evidence bags and the bedroom, I'd stopped asking how to catch her…and started wondering how to keep her safe.

What to hide.

What to burn.

What to rewrite before anyone else saw the truth I already knew.

Motive, Means, and Morris | Isabella

Alexis dumped a small box on my table. "I've got it."

I glanced up. "Got what?"

"The method. For Ty." When she flipped open the box I saw no blueprints, no gun. Just a small prescription bottle in a zip lock bag, labeled with a fake pharmacy tag. Inside were a few white pills and a folded notepad.

"Fentanyl," she said, tapping the bottle. "Not street junk. Medical grade. My cousin does disposal runs for a pain clinic. He clears out expired samples, abandoned prescriptions, that kind of thing."

I frowned. "And he just gave it to you?"

"He didn't ask," she said. "He thinks I needed it for a scare tactic. 'Scare him straight,' I said. He's nosy, not stupid. But he minds his business."

"Fentanyl's everywhere. No one questions it anymore. Dust a little on the rim of his water bottle. He takes a sip at the gym. Dead before he hits the floor."

I swallowed. "You're sure that'll work?"

"I've researched it. I know the dose. I know how fast it works." She gave me a grim smile. "He won't feel a thing—just one last workout, then lights out."

"This isn't a science project."

"No shit B. You think I don't know that?"

I stared at her "This is something you can't come back from. I'm worried."

"It's something you couldn't come back from," she shot back. I flinched.

"I'm not trying to be mean, but you can't talk me out of this either."

Her voice cracked on the last word. Just enough to remind me this wasn't vengeance. This was necessity.

She tapped the folder. "This plan doesn't involve rage. Or chaos. Or blood. It just looks like fate finally caught up with him."

It wasn't my style. That was the point. Alexis didn't want to become me.

"And the setup?" I asked.

"I've been watching him for days. He always carries a shaker bottle in his gym bag. One scoop of pre-workout. Easy to swap. I've got the gloves, the mask, everything."

I exhaled slowly, nodding. "You've thought of everything."

"Almost everything," she said.

A knock at the door cut through the moment like a scalpel.

I moved quietly to the peephole, every nerve on high alert. Not Eli.

A man in plainclothes. Early forties. Calm face..

"Morris," I whispered. "Cold case detective."

Alexis's posture shifted. "Want me to stay?"

"No. Back room. Just in case."

She vanished without another word.

I opened the door halfway. "Can I help you?"

He held up a badge. "Detective Morris. Just following up on a cold case. Connor Maddox."

My stomach flipped. "That was years ago."

"Cold cases don't expire," he said easily. "Sometimes it takes time for the truth to get uncomfortable enough to show itself."

I said nothing.

"You knew him," he continued, voice light. "We've got old school photos. Texts. History. Figured I'd stop by, see if you remembered anything…interesting."

I kept my face neutral. "I didn't even know he was dead until someone told me after graduation."

"Still," he said, letting the silence linger like bait, "you dated him once, didn't you?"

"A long time ago."

"Can still leave big marks."

I stepped back. "What exactly are you implying, Detective?"

He smiled like it didn't matter. "Nothing. Just following threads. Asking around. You'd be surprised how often patterns hide in hindsight."

He reached into his jacket and pulled out a card, setting it on the table just inside the door.

"If you remember anything. Even something small."

I didn't move to take it. "Is that all?"

"For now." He gave a brief nod toward the hallway. "Nice place. Quiet. Hope it stays that way."

I shut the door and double-locked it. Alexis emerged from the back, her expression stormy. "He was fishing."

I nodded. "And I'm the bait."

Her eyes narrowed. " What happened?"

I hesitated, then said it anyway. "A detective showed up. Cold case. He's asking questions about…someone I used to know."

We stood in silence for a long minute, the weight of it settling on our shoulders like a trap.

Alexis picked up the folder again. "Then we don't wait."

I looked at the pill bottle. She was ready. And I was out of time.

"We do it tonight," I said, my voice low.

Her eyes narrowed. "Yup, tonight," she said staring back at me.

"If Morris is starting with Connor," I said, "he's going to reach the rest. Maybe not today. Maybe not this week. But it's coming."

The Tipping Point | Alexis

Ty showed up this morning.
There was no text, no call, no apology. Just his fist slamming into the door like he still had keys to my life. And the sad thing was, he did—literally. I'd forgotten about the spare in the flowerpot on the porch. By the time I realized it, he was already in the living room, standing there like he owned the place, holding up his duffel bag like it was some peace offering.

"I think we should talk," he said like it was reasonable. Like the last time we spoke hadn't ended with me screaming at him to get out and never come back. "You left things messy."

No. He left things messy. He left *me* a mess. But of course, he wouldn't take responsibility. He never did.

I didn't argue. I went into autopilot—because that's what fear does. It freezes you. It makes you small. And I'd already wasted too much of my life being small around him.

By lunch, I was texting Bell.

She met me in the teacher's lot behind the school. She didn't ask me to explain anything. Just opened her bag and handed me a small prescription bottle tucked in a zip lock, the kind that could pass as allergy meds if someone wasn't paying attention. The envelope was thicker than I expected, heavy with forged statements, a therapist's note, even a typed suicide letter in a font that looked a little too perfect.

"Are you sure?" she asked, not because she thought I'd change my mind—but because she wanted me to own it.

I nodded. "Yeah. I'm sure."

"Then make it look like he did it to himself," she said, already turning away.

By the time I got home, Ty was in the shower. Steam rolled out from under the door, his voice echoing some off-key melody. The scent of his body wash filled the hallway, and my stomach turned.

I opened the bottle, crushed three of the pills between the back of a spoon and the counter's edge, and stirred the powder into the pasta sauce I'd started that morning. It dissolved fast, easy, like it had never existed.

When he came out, towel low, grinning like we were still playing house, he looked at the plate I set down for him and smiled. "Damn, you're cooking now?"

I sat across from him and picked at my food, watching as he shoveled it was nothing.

"Everything tastes better when you make it," he said, licking sauce from his fingers. "I swear, I missed this."

He said it like he meant it. Like he really believed the version of reality he was selling. But I wasn't buying.

A few bites later, he slowed. Blinked hard. Drank water, then coughed once. Twice. His face tightened in confusion.

"Something's off," he muttered. "You feel hot in here?"

I just sat back, folding my hands in my lap. "No. Feels normal to me."

His brow creased, and then his hand went to his chest. He tried to stand, but his balance betrayed him. The fork clattered to the floor, and he looked at me with wide, searching eyes.

"What did you—what's happening?"

"You came back," I said evenly, not moving from my chair. "That's what happened."

He opened his mouth like he was going to beg or threaten—maybe both—but words didn't make it out. His legs gave out. He dropped to the floor, gasping, a panic rising behind his eyes that was almost familiar. The same kind I'd had when he used to scream in my face, when he'd yank my phone from my hand mid-text or accuse me of things I hadn't done.

Now the fear was his. And I felt nothing.

I stood slowly, walked around the table, and knelt beside him. His lips were moving, but I didn't care what he was saying. The details didn't matter. I brushed my fingers over his cheek like a goodbye.

"You made me afraid to sleep," I whispered. "Afraid to breathe. You took my voice. This isn't revenge. This is release."

His hand twitched once before going limp.

He was gone.

No violent thrashing. No blood. Just stillness.

I watched for a moment longer, just to be sure, then rose and moved to the sink. I washed the dishes methodically. Cleaned up the counters. Made it all look like a normal evening.

Then I slid the envelope from Bell under the couch cushion, just far enough to be found but not staged. Inside it was the narrative—the false trail of declining mental health, a suggestion of substance use, the implied tragedy that happens too often in silence. When the detectives came, they'd see exactly what they were supposed to see: a man who fell apart and couldn't put himself back together.

Before leaving, I sent Bell one text.

It's done. You were right. I didn't flinch.
Her reply came minutes later.
Clean up. I've got the rest.
I zipped up my hoodie, stepped over his body, and walked out. The air outside was biting, but it didn't faze me. I walked around the block three times, until the cold burned my lungs in a way that felt like breathing again.

There wasn't guilt. No wave of regret. Just clarity. Stillness. And underneath it, something else—low, dark, and pulsing like a second heartbeat.

Bell never explained what it felt like. But I've seen it in her—in the way her voice goes flat when she talks about men like Ty. In the silence she wears like armor. I didn't understand it before.

I do now.

It's not a craving. It's more like a door once opened that you can't close again. A part of yourself that doesn't vanish once it wakes up. And I know, without any fear or shame, that I won't be the one to close it.

Like Nothing Ever Happened | Isabella

Alexis made waffles. She whisked the batter by hand, poured it into the iron with practiced care, and even warmed the syrup on the stove like we were hosting brunch instead of trying to keep blood off our hands. She moved around the kitchen like she had nothing to hide, like last week hadn't ended with her staging a death and texting me with a steady hand. Everything about her this morning radiated calm, like she'd stepped into some new version of herself that didn't include panic or guilt.

I hadn't meant to stay the night, but when she texted me late—*"Can you crash here? Just in case?"*—I couldn't say no. Maybe I wanted to keep an eye on her. Maybe I didn't trust that she wouldn't unravel quietly. Or maybe, deep down, I just needed to see what it looked like when someone walked away from the life and didn't flinch.

Now I sat at the counter nursing a cup of black coffee that had long gone cold, watching her hum along to an upbeat playlist like it was just another Saturday. From the outside, anyone walking in might've believed she was celebrating something.

"You want whipped cream?" she asked, not bothering to look up as she finished plating.

Her voice held the same lightness it always had when she

was teasing or bored. The question came so casually, so easily, it took me a second too long to answer.

"Sure," I replied.

She added a perfect swirl and slid the plate across the counter to me. I looked down at the food, then back at her, trying to understand how she was sitting so comfortably inside this aftermath. A week ago, she was crying in my car, begging for a way out, shaking. Now she was flipping waffles and asking about whipped cream like nothing had happened at all.

"Did you sleep?" I asked, my voice quieter than I intended.

"Like a rock," she said around a bite, licking syrup from her lip. "Honestly, best sleep I've had in months. I think my body finally caught up to my brain."

I wanted to ask her what that meant, but I already knew. Her Something inside her had aligned. Whatever she'd done had cracked her open and set her right. Meanwhile, I felt like I was splintering, piece by piece, with every hour Eli didn't call.

He hadn't shown up. Not once. He hadn't texted since the press release two days ago, the one that declared Ty Vaughn's death a tragic overdose, ruled accidental with no signs of foul play. It was everything we wanted. Everything Alexis had planned. It worked.

But something about the way it *worked* felt like a trap. Too easy. Too final. Like the lie had buried something real, and Eli could smell the dirt.

Alexis left shortly after breakfast, back to her usual rhythm, makeup done, jacket slung over one shoulder like the world didn't carry weight anymore. She blew me a kiss before walking out the door, promised to bring smoothies on the way home, and disappeared.

I left ten minutes later and drove straight to the precinct. I didn't text first.

When I walked into the squad room, Eli was at his desk, sleeves rolled up, jaw tight, eyes narrowed at whatever was in the folder before him. He didn't look up immediately, which gave me too much time to study him. He looked older.

"You're not supposed to be here," he said without turning his head.

"I'm not following rules today."

His jaw flexed. "You usually don't."

I stepped inside, letting the door close behind me. "Is this what we're doing now? Radio silence?"

"You tell me," he said, finally looking up. His voice was calm, but the kind of calm that held back a storm.

I crossed my arms. "I don't know what you want me to say."

"Then don't say anything."

The weight of his eyes on me made it impossible to breathe properly. I used to feel safe when he looked at me. Now it felt like I was under a microscope, each flaw laid bare under the scrutiny of someone who once believed in me and wasn't sure if he still did.

"Eli," I said carefully, "if there's something you're not saying—"

"There's a lot I'm not saying." He stood, slowly, his movements were guarded now. "Because if I start, I won't stop."

I swallowed hard. "I don't want you to stop."

He stepped around the desk and leaned against the edge of it, arms folded. "I can't keep pretending I don't see the way everything around you bends."

I didn't move.

"You walk through chaos like it's home, and every time I think I understand who you are, something shifts." His voice didn't rise, but it got sharper. "You don't flinch, Bell. Not when you should. Not when most people would."

"Does that scare you?"

Eli's gaze didn't waver. "No. But it makes me wonder what else you're capable of."

My heart thudded.

He wasn't accusing me. He wasn't pulling out evidence or asking direct questions. But he was laying down a line in the sand.

"I never asked you to understand everything," I said.

"No," he agreed, "but you let me fall anyway."

That one landed. Right between the ribs.

"I didn't mean to."

He looked down, hands pressing against the desk behind him like he needed it to stay upright. "You didn't have to mean it. It still happened."

The silence stretched.

I wanted to grab his hand and pull us both back from the edge. But the gap between us wasn't physical—it was the weight of everything I hadn't said, the truths I'd let sit unspoken, and the decisions I'd made without giving him the chance to know me fully.

"I'm not asking you to fix me," I said finally.

"Good," he replied, eyes steady on mine. "Because I'm not sure I can."

The finality in his tone didn't come with anger. It came with something worse—resignation.

He wasn't slamming doors or drawing conclusions. But he was closing something quietly, and the sound of it made my chest tighten in a way I couldn't explain.

I nodded once. "Thanks for not saying the thing you're

thinking."

"I figured you already knew."

I turned toward the door. "I did."

His fingers drummed once against the edge of the desk. Then he stood, slow and stiff like his body wasn't entirely his anymore.

"Bell."

I paused, half-turned.

He didn't soften. "The case is shifting. Someone came forward this morning with a new name, a new connection. It's not solid, but it's enough to muddy the water—and it means I'm not the only one watching anymore."

I felt the floor shift under me, even though my feet stayed planted.

"What kind of connection?" I asked, carefully.

"A name that's been near every fire I've followed," he said, eyes narrowing slightly. "But not yours."

I stayed quiet, afraid to guess.

"I'm telling you this once," Eli said. "If you want to walk away from all of it—really walk—I'll give you that chance. I'll handle whatever falls out from the next phase of the investigation. But if you keep doing this… You cannot keep doing this."

I stared at him. The weight of it hung there, thick and final.

"I'm not asking you to confess," he added. "I'm not even asking for honesty. But I'm not stupid, Bell. And you're running out of corners to hide in."

He turned back to his desk, picked up a pen, and started scribbling something I couldn't see. Like I'd already left.

And maybe, in a way, I had.

Like Freedom | Isabella

I watched the light crawl across my kitchen floor, slicing through the blinds in soft lines that turned gold and then gray against the hardwood. My coffee had gone cold in the chipped mug I kept meaning to replace but never did. A playlist hummed in the background—something mellow and familiar—but I wasn't really listening. My head was too full of Eli's voice.

I'm telling you this once. If you want to walk away from all of it—really walk—I'll give you that chance.

He'd just offered an exit like he wasn't sure I'd take it. And the strange thing was, I wasn't sure either. For once, I wasn't scanning for cameras or checking who might be watching. I wasn't waiting for the next name to show up in a file or the next gut-deep pull to remind me who I'd become. I was just... sitting still.

I sat at the counter, mug in hand, letting the quiet fill every inch of my apartment. I stared at a folded dish towel for longer than I'd admit. This place was lived in but untouched, like someone else's life was there. There were no signs of who I used to be. No weapons in the closet. No getaway bags in the coat cabinet. No late-night prep sessions with black gloves and burner phones.

What was left was just me—and the truth I'd been circling for weeks.

I hadn't crossed the final line. But I'd stood on the edge. I'd watched the wind blow across it, daring me to step over. And I hadn't. Not because I was afraid. But because Eli had asked the question no one else had: *what happens if you just stop?*

That stayed with me.

The thing that kept me up wasn't guilt. It was proximity. The almost. The fact that I could have gone further—and didn't. The way Eli looked at me with something close to heartbreak. He didn't want the facts. He wanted a decision.

If I was going to choose anything, it had to be him. Not because he deserved a cleaned-up version of me. Not because he asked. But because I couldn't imagine waking up in a world where he looked at me like a stranger. Because I love him.

I didn't tell anyone where I was going. I didn't even take my phone off airplane mode. I just drove—no destination, no plan. The city slipped past in a blur of stoplights and sidewalk chatter. Familiar landmarks shifted in meaning. The corner store where Eli once handed me a ginger ale and called it a peace offering. The bridge where we talked until the sky turned lavender. The intersection where we fought like the air itself was thick with loss.

I ended up at the overlook. The one just past the last bus stop, where the cracked pavement threatened to give way if you leaned too far. There was nothing scenic about it. No perfect skyline or poetic view. Just an expanse of city and silence.

I got out of the car and leaned against the hood, arms folded. The wind pressed against my sleeves like it was trying to carry something away from me. For once, I let it.

I thought about how long I'd been in survival mode. How sharp I'd become. How the killing never felt like justice or power—just control. A way to keep the panic at bay. A way to stay one step ahead of feelings. But Eli made me feel it all. And I hated him for that. And I loved him more because of it.

He was the variable I couldn't calculate. The one thing that didn't fit in any box, didn't respond to any of the rules. He made me question the armor. Not by breaking it, but by standing still and waiting to see if I'd take it off myself.

And I did.

When I got home, I didn't make a list. I didn't overthink it. I just moved.

I started in the bathroom, false-bottom drawer emptied. Gloves, blades, wipes—all dumped into the duffel bag I used to keep packed under the bed. In the closet, I pulled the folder of surveillance notes and old kill files. I fed them through the shredder until it groaned and overheated.

The burner phone went next. Battery ripped out. SIM cracked. I stomped on the plastic with my boot and buried the pieces in a trash bag beneath takeout containers and last week's receipts.

Last was the key-shaped blade. I held it in my palm, waiting to feel that surge of connection or nostalgia or control. It didn't come. All I felt was the cold weight of something I no longer needed.

I wrapped it in a kitchen towel and slid it into the duffel. I couldn't throw it away yet. But I didn't want it near me either.

By the time I zipped the bag shut and pushed it under the bed, the apartment felt… different. Not cleansed. Not pure. But quieter.

I made tea and sat back down at the counter. Opened a

book I'd started three times and never finished. The words blurred, but I didn't mind. I wasn't reading for distraction. I just wanted to sit in the stillness a little longer.

Outside, the city kept moving.

Still Bleeding | Isabella

I didn't wear black.
Black was for mourning. For endings. And I wasn't ready to dress like something had died.

I kept it simple—jeans, a worn hoodie, sneakers that didn't make a sound when I walked. I didn't rehearse the perfect speech. I just drove until I reached the one place I hadn't let myself go in days.

Eli's apartment sat like a question at the end of a quiet cul-de-sac, tucked behind a row of wind-stripped sycamores. His car was there. The lights were on. And still, I hesitated.

What did you say to someone who had seen you—really seen you—and still hadn't decided if he was staying?

I didn't knock like a girl trying to charm her way back in. I knocked like someone who owed a reckoning.

When the door opened, Eli didn't look surprised. If anything, he looked…tired. Like he'd been waiting for me longer than he wanted to admit.

We stood there, just staring for a breath too long.

Finally, he stepped back. "You cold?"

"Only a little."

The door shut behind me with a soft click, and for a moment, it was just the hum of his fridge and the sound of my heartbeat.

"I'm not here to lie to you," I said, voice steady but low. "Or to explain things you've already decided not to ask about."

Eli leaned against the kitchen counter, arms crossed. "That's good. Because I'm not sure I could stand to hear them."

I nodded. "Fair."

He studied me in silence, like he was still taking inventory of the parts I hadn't revealed yet.

"I'm not who I was," I said. "But I'm trying to figure it out now. And if there's any part of you that still thinks I'm worth knowing, then I need you to understand something."

Eli didn't move, but his expression shifted slightly. "Say it."

I took a breath.

"I didn't stay because I didn't care. I stayed because I didn't know who I was without it. That part of me—the cold, quiet, clinical part—it made sense. Until you didn't."

He blinked. "What does that mean?"

"It means you're the only thing that ever made me hesitate."

His jaw tightened.

"I don't need forgiveness," I said. "I'm not even asking for it. I just…wanted you to see me now. The version that chose not to keep going."

Eli was still for a long moment. Then, almost imperceptibly, he nodded. Just once.

He didn't speak. But he stepped forward, the gap between us closing one slow inch at a time. When he finally touched me—his hand grazing mine like he wasn't sure he had permission—I let him. I let myself lean into that quiet gravity we always circled.

Eli's fingers threaded through mine, and he let out a breath that sounded more like surrender than relief.

"Come here," he whispered.

His mouth met mine with that slow, searching hunger—the kind that wasn't about sex or possession, but confirmation. His hands moved to my waist, grounding me. Mine slid beneath the hem of his shirt, needing to feel skin, heat, heartbeat. Anything real.

When I pulled it over his head and dropped it to the floor, he didn't flinch. He just kissed me harder. Slower. Like he was memorizing this version of me. The one who wasn't armored.

I pulled off my hoodie next, then my shirt, until we were skin against skin, chest to chest, with nothing but air and electricity between us.

Silently, he walked me backward toward the bedroom, lips still on mine, one hand resting on my lower back as if he wasn't ready to let me go. When we reached the edge of the bed, I sat, then lay back, watching him as he knelt over me, hands planted on either side of my hips.

The tension between us was still there, but it had shifted—no longer something we were bracing against, but something we were finally, fully letting go.

Eli kissed down the slope of my neck, past my collarbone, then paused just above the swell of my chest. He looked up at me.

"I thought I lost you," he murmured, voice rough.

"You didn't."

He lowered his head again, kissing over my sternum, then lower, across the center of my stomach. I lifted my hips just enough for him to slip my jeans down, his hands slow, tracing the shape of my thighs like he hadn't decided whether to hold me or worship me.

I wasn't used to being touched like this. Not gently. Not without some kind of transaction built in. But Eli didn't ask for anything. He just gave.

When he finally settled between my legs, I gasped—soft at first, then louder as his mouth pressed into me. He wasn't in a rush. His tongue moved in smooth, practiced strokes, one hand holding my hip in place while the other slid up my ribs, grounding me again.

My fingers tangled in his hair, and I felt myself unraveling—not just from the pressure building in my core, but from the pressure I'd carried for too long. It broke open inside me.

When I came, I bit my lip so hard I tasted blood. He stayed with me through the tremors, kissing my inner thigh before rising again, eyes dark, mouth shining.

"Get up here," I whispered, pulling him by the waistband of his jeans.

He stripped them off in one smooth motion, boxers too, then covered my body with his like he was afraid I'd vanish.

He didn't slam into me.

He pushed in slowly, deliberately, watching every inch disappear like it mattered. Like I mattered.

I wrapped my legs around his waist, anchoring us together. We moved in rhythm—not fast, not frantic. Like we'd waited for this moment and weren't in any hurry to let it go.

Eli kissed me like he'd never stopped. I clung to him, to the weight of his body, the sound of his breathing, the feel of his hands threading through mine and pinning them to the mattress.

When he finally let go, it wasn't with a grunt or a curse. It was with my name, whispered like a prayer against my cheek.

We didn't speak for a long time after. Just lay there, tangled, our limbs a quiet apology for everything we hadn't handled gently before.

Eventually, his hand found mine again.
"You came back," he murmured.
I turned to face him, brushing the hair from his forehead.
"I never left."

The Ones Who Walk Away | Eli

The precinct felt quieter than usual, though the noise hadn't changed. Phones still rang. Radios buzzed. Someone in the back laughed too hard at something that probably wasn't funny. But to me, everything felt muffled—like I'd already started slipping out of place.

Captain Matthews called me into his office before I even got my second cup of coffee. He didn't bother with pleasantries.

"We've got something hot coming in from City Hall," he said, sliding a red-tabbed file across the desk. "DA's office wants it sealed up fast and quiet. They requested you."

I opened the folder. Councilman Shaw. Found unconscious in a high-end hotel suite with a cocktail of drugs and someone who didn't match his marriage license.

"They want plausible deniability," he added. "No leaks. No missteps."

I nodded. "You pulling me off the other one?"

"You were dancing in circles anyway. Spencer can pick up whatever crumbs are left. I need you focused on this. Starting now."

I tucked the file under my arm and left without asking for clarification.

At my desk, I stared down at the other folder. The one

that had lived too long in the bottom of my go-bag. Inside were unfilled notes, flagged search histories, half-buried names. Nothing substantial. But enough to point in a direction. If anyone looked too closely.

The truth was, I never intended to turn it in.

I slipped the folder into my backpack and zipped it shut. Then I powered down my monitor, took my badge off the hook, and slid it into my pocket.

Jason passed by with two energy drinks and a bag of trail mix. He didn't stop, but he gave me a look.

"Matthews said you're off it?"

"Yeah," I said, slinging the backpack over my shoulder.

"Guess I'm stuck chasing shadows, then," he muttered.

"You'll make them talk," I said.

He nodded once. "You've been wound tight lately. Thought you were gonna start bunking here."

"Couch's too stiff," I said. "Even for me."

He grinned and walked off, fading back into the controlled chaos of the bullpen.

I walked out without looking back.

I didn't know if I'd burn the folder tonight or bury it. But I knew it would never make it into evidence.

And that, for the first time, felt like the right call.

* * *

Morris caught me just as I was heading down the steps, his coat collar flipped up against the wind, his expression unreadable beneath the brim of his hat. He didn't smile. Just stood there, sizing me up like he was deciding whether to speak or walk away.

"New case?" he asked, his eyes flicking toward the folder tucked under my arm.

I nodded once. "City Hall wants it cleaned up fast. Discreet. No room for noise or leaks."

He tilted his head slightly, as if weighing whether or not to believe me. Then he said, "They picked the right guy."

We stood in the middle of the sidewalk for a few seconds, neither of us moving, the moment stretching out long enough to carry weight.

"You know," he said finally, voice low and even, "sometimes a pattern leads you somewhere. Brings clarity. But other times… it just loops. You keep following it, hoping it breaks. But it never does."

"You think that's what this was?" I asked.

He gave a small shrug. "I kept seeing the same names surface around the same edges. Same smoke. But the fire's gone now. If there's no heat left—there's no case left either."

Morris stepped back, pulling his coat tighter against the wind. "I talked to people," he said simply. "Old friends. A girl Connor used to see. Even a campus TA who caught them arguing once."

I didn't speak. Just waited.

"They all said the same thing—he had a temper. Knew how to push. How to intimidate. One said she saw bruises on her once. Said Bell laughed it off."

His eyes met mine, sharp beneath the brim of his hat.

"She's not clean. I know that. But clean and guilty aren't the same thing. I'm not chasing shadows," he added. "And I'm not wasting time dragging in people who've already been hurt enough."

He didn't wait for a reply. Just tipped his chin and turned to walk off.

"That what you think I'm doing?" I called after him.

He paused, and turned back to me. "I think you made your choice. And I think if anything starts up again—if someone pushes too far—I'll be waiting."

That night, I found myself driving without direction, until the overlook pulled me in like gravity. Bell was already there, perched on the hood of her car with her boots crossed at the ankle, her hoodie pulled up. She didn't look over when I parked or when I joined her. She just stared out over the glow of the city, like she was still waiting for it to give her answers she wasn't brave enough to ask.

I climbed onto the hood beside her.

"You okay?" I asked, voice low, the wind slipping between us like breath.

"Getting there."

We sat in the quiet, shoulder to shoulder, letting the air between us settle into something that felt like understanding. I looked over at her, watched the way the city lights caught the curve of her jaw and the quiet steel in her expression.

"I'm off it," I said softly.

She glanced at me, unsurprising. "You sure?"

"Yeah."

She turned to face me more fully, eyes steady. "So what now?"

I exhaled, then looked out over the skyline, letting the weight of everything we weren't saying land exactly where it needed to.

"We stop running," I said. "We start choosing."

She didn't smile. But she didn't look away either.

And for the first time in what felt like forever, we both stayed

still—no escape routes, no lies, no need to hide.
Just quiet. Just breath. Just us.

Epilogue | Isabella

The quiet held longer than I expected.

The city kept moving, same as always—headlines full of scandals, celebrity overdoses, and political implosions that had nothing to do with me. No new bodies. No strange calls. No reports that hinted at patterns buried beneath the surface. It wasn't peace exactly.

Eli was steady again—up before sunrise, black coffee in hand, solving cases that didn't feel like they were tracing our footsteps. We didn't talk about what we were anymore. We just were. Something between comfort and unfinished business.

I started sleeping through the night.

The box under my bed stayed where I left it. I hadn't opened it since the night I packed everything away—wipes, gloves, the blade, all the tools that used to make me feel prepared. I didn't touch them. Knowing they were sealed tight in the dark, out of reach, was enough.

Until this morning.

I wasn't looking for anything dangerous. Just an old hoodie I hadn't worn in months. But when I slid my hand under the bed and brushed my fingers across the zipper, something felt off.

I pulled the box out slowly and unzipped it.

EPILOGUE | ISABELLA

Nothing was missing, but everything was slightly off. The blade was no longer centered in the towel—it had shifted, just barely. The cloth was looser. The tight, sealed air of the box had been disturbed. It smelled…opened. Briefly. Carefully. Not by accident.

I didn't panic.

I didn't scream.

But I didn't feel steady either.

I stared at the blade for a long moment. It still looked the same—cold, quiet, familiar. The kind of tool that didn't forget its purpose even when you did.

Not to warn me. Not to threaten anything. Just to make sure it was still there—intact, untouched. Like she needed to confirm something for herself. Or maybe for me.

And I wasn't sure what unsettled me more—the idea that she'd come back…

…or the fact that I wasn't surprised.

Note to My Readers

Thank you for walking this line with Isabella.

She wasn't built to be a heroine in shining armor—or a villain with a perfect plan. She was made to survive, to adapt, and to choose. Sometimes, that choice isn't about redemption. It's about letting go of what no longer fits, even if it once felt like safety.

This story was never about perfection. It was about proximity—the tension between who we are and who we could be if someone really saw us.

For Eli, it was about looking at the truth and not flinching.

For Alexis...well, some stories keep writing themselves even after the last page.

If this book left you breathless, unsettled, or even just understood—I hope you know that's exactly the point. Thank you for reading, for feeling, for following the shadows to their edge.

If Isabella ever comes back?

You'll be the first to know.

—Ashley Johnson

Note from the author

Thank you for walking this line with Isabella. She wasn't built to be a heroine in shining armor—or a villain with a perfect plan. She was made to survive, to adapt, and to choose. Sometimes, that choice isn't about redemption. It's about letting go of what no longer fits, even if it once felt like safety. This story was never about perfection. It was about proximity—the tension between who we are and who we could be if someone really saw us. For Eli, it was about looking at the truth and not flinching. For Alexis…well, some stories keep writing themselves even after the last page. If this book left you breathless, unsettled, or even just understood—I hope you know that's exactly the point. Thank you for reading, for feeling, for following the shadows to their edge. If Isabella ever comes back? You'll be the first to know.
—Ashley Johnson

www.ingramcontent.com/pod-product-compliance
Lightning Source LLC
LaVergne TN
LVHW041931070526
838199LV00051BA/2771